"Don't count on us being friends, Mr. Pritchard."

"Oh, now, don't be so stiff. I'm just plain Harry."

"To your friends?" Felicia said mockingly.

He laughed. "I'm Harry to my enemies, too." He shook his head. "I'll leave my door open in case you get frightened or just want to talk. I overheard about your mother. I'm sorry."

Pain flickered in Felicia's eyes. Harry sighed. He hated vulnerability in women. He always noticed it and felt obliged to do something. It wasn't too often he got thanked for his trouble, either. He obviously wasn't doing something right.

He looked down for a heartbeat, then lifted his head and met Felicia's gaze again. "We are going to be friends. We have a lot in common. We're both pigheaded and jump to conclusions. And on that note..." He shifted his duffle to his shoulder. "See you around, neighbor."

ABOUT THE AUTHOR

Jackie Weger loves to travel to research the fascinating places and professions that inspire the stories she shares with her readers. She was born in Mobile, Alabama, and has lived in half a dozen states so far. Currently, she and her husband live in St. Augustine, Florida.

Books by Jackie Weger

HARLEQUIN AMERICAN ROMANCE

HARLEQUIN TEMPTATION

HARLEQUIN SUPERROMANCE

Don't miss any of our special offers. Write to us at the following address for information on our newest releases.

Harlequin Reader Service
901 Fuhrmann Blvd., P.O. Box 1397, Buffalo, NY 14240
Canadian address: P.O. Box 603,

JACKIE WEGER

FIRST IMPRESSIONS

Harlequin Books

TORONTO • NEW YORK • LONDON
AMSTERDAM • PARIS • SYDNEY • HAMBURG
STOCKHOLM • ATHENS • TOKYO • MILAN

Many thanks to
C.E. Bent & Sons, Inc., floatbuilders
and Rose Parade float designers,
for all their help

Published October 1990

ISBN 0-373-16363-0

Chapter One

Felicia watched the taxi pull away from the curb. She had overtipped the cabbie. A subconscious gesture, she thought. Perhaps because she was glad to be home.

In only a few seconds she would be among her own things, in her own space—alone as she had never before been alone in her life.

Home. Pasadena, California, in the San Gabriel Valley.

During the Great Depression, long before she'd been born, a quality-of-life study had rated it as the best U.S. city in which to live. Most residents still agreed. It was a city with a rich past, best known worldwide for its annual extravaganza, the Rose Parade, which boasted a television audience of 350 million in thirty-two countries.

The thought of an audience of such magnitude gave Felicia chills: for each of the past five years, up to three of those Rose Parade floats had been of her design. And in the roundtable drafts held this February, her designs had won contracts for *five* floats.

She knew she was making a name for herself in the float-building industry. But at the moment all of her energy was devoted to coping with the present. Float designing and winning trophys seemed distant and unreal. She was alone.

Her mind grasped for the meaning of *aloneness*. Abandoned. Orphaned. Could a twenty-nine-year-old woman be orphaned? No, not in the strictest sense of the word. But her heart said yes.

The leaden feeling in the pit of her stomach had begun as she'd watched her mother's casket being lowered into the earth. She just couldn't seem to shake the feeling. She had no brothers, sisters, aunts, uncles or cousins. No father, and now, no mother. She had not a single soul with whom to share her failures and triumphs.

She couldn't pick up the phone anymore and say "Mom! I had the most fantastic date last night," or "Mom! My float design won the National Trophy!" or "Mom! I picked up a few extra dollars on a side job. I'm flying home this weekend."

And home was no longer a modest, wood-framed house in Mill Creek surrounded by the soaring trees of Lassen National Forest. The house had been sold weeks ago to cover medical bills accumulated over the course of her mother's illness.

Felicia sighed. Home was now the beige stucco apartment building in which she had lived for the past five years.

As she looked around, she noticed dust settling up and down Catalina Street. Pedestrians were bending to retrieve packages and purses. In front of the building across the street, a woman was sweeping up broken glass.

There had been an earthquake.

She had not noticed. One of the oddest phenomena of earthquakes was that if one were riding in a car, one did not feel the tremor. Unless, of course, it was so violent that roads cracked, parted and swallowed the car, or dumped it off the freeway.

In her present frame of mind, Felicia thought wryly, she probably would not have noticed even that.

She'd read somewhere that after the death of his father a man was immutably a man. So, after a woman's mother died, did that make her immutably a woman?

Felicia didn't think so. Expelling another sigh, she hefted her suitcases and stepped into the entrance hall.

At once she was flagged down by one of the elderly tenants. Felicia winced inwardly. The problem with Lila Ross was that Lila often spoke fluent gibberish and could take an hour doing it. Felicia's own mother's mind often "travelled" at the last. Had nurses and caretakers felt as silently impatient with her mother as she, herself, now did with Lila? Felicia wondered. Feeling sudden compassion and a stab of guilt, she put down her luggage.

"What is it, Lila?"

"Please help me," the old woman pleaded. "The door is stuck. I was in the garden when the quake struck. My birds! My poor little tweeties! I just know their cage toppled."

Felicia held out her hand for the key. "Let me try it."

Suddenly cautious, Lila's eyes darted away and back, as if having difficulty focusing on Felicia's face. "I know you, don't I?"

"Of course you do." Felicia's voice was soothing. She touched Lila on the shoulder. "I'm Felicia Bennington. I live upstairs, apartment six, but I've been out of—''

"Oh, now I remember, you're the artist."

"Sort of. I design—''

"Clare introduced us, didn't she?" Lila's face glowed, proud of her recall. "I like Clare."

"Yes, she did," Felicia confirmed, smiling, determined to stand there and listen patiently. Lila placed the key in her open palm. It slid easily into the lock and clicked.

"There now," Felicia said, pushing. The door stayed firmly closed.

"I was in the garden when the ground came up," repeated Lila. "The bench broke in half. Mr. Cooper will think I broke it. But I didn't."

Felicia let the babble go in one ear and out the other. "It's not the lock. The door is jammed. These old buildings..." She put her shoulder against the door and pushed. The door refused to budge. "Damn!''

"May I help?" came a deep resonant voice.

"Oh, please," trilled Lila. "I'm certain my poor birds are frightened. Maybe even dead." She began to cry. "I don't like dead, I don't like dead, I don't—''

"Of course your birds aren't dead," Felicia said, trying to calm the elderly woman.

The man dropped a duffle bag to the floor and moved between her and Lila.

"Step back a little more," he directed. Felicia complied. Lila, tears streaming, hovered.

With her artist's eyes, Felicia observed the man's profile. He had a lean, almost thin face offset by a full lower lip and cleft chin. His hair was dark auburn and curly. Somewhat unkempt, it was long on his nape as if he had skipped a haircut. He was unshaven, but not bearded, and had the prerequisite California tan. In the dusky hall light he appeared to be in his mid-thirties.

Reaching up, he thumped the door with the side of a balled fist from top edge to lock, then he gave it a resounding thwack. The door flew open to reveal that the heavy bird cage had indeed toppled over. Seed was scattered across the floor, the birds chirping in panic from one corner of the cage.

"Oh, no!" Lila wailed as she rushed inside.

"Wait," Felicia told her. "I'll help you lift it."

"No!" Lila spun around with surprising agility, throwing her arms wide to prevent Felicia's entry. Her voice shifted lower. "I can do it myself."

The door slammed closed.

Felicia stared blankly at it for a few seconds. Then, remembering the man, she turned to thank him for his help, to explain Lila's behavior.

He was gone.

With a shake of her head she retrieved her suitcases. "Good deeds are done for yourself—not others," her mother had often said. "Never stand around waiting for a thank you. It might not be forthcoming." Right again, Mom, Felicia thought, as she dragged her luggage up the stairs.

She longed for a quick soak in the tub, a cup of strong hot tea and then bed. She could unpack her suitcases tomorrow; unpack too, all the family memories that threatened to flood her.

Her own apartment door was ajar.

Felicia's heart skipped a beat, fear erasing weariness.

Now, wait a minute, she warned herself. Don't panic. During quakes doors get stuck and doors fly open. And ceiling fixtures fall down, she noted, glancing at the hall light, dangling unlit from its wires. Bits of ceiling plaster dusted the dark, tiled floor.

The situation required caution, not panic.

She pushed the door back until it met the wall. Her hand snaked inside to flip the light switch. She could see almost the whole of her apartment. There was her drafting table upright by the window, safe as it could be. The television set was in place. Below it on the shelf was the small stereo. Scattered across the floor were scores of colored pens and pencils. Magazines had fallen from the coffee table, a lamp was overturned, the shade at a rakish angle.

Minor quake damage, Felicia thought. Nothing more. Still . . .

She knocked loudly on the doorjamb.

"Anybody home? I'm just checking to see if everyone is all right."

The inquiry was met with silence. *Okay*, she thought, *it made me feel stupid, but I did it by the book*. She crossed the threshold. Kitchen cabinets were open, though none of their contents had spilled out. She crossed the living room and entered the bedroom.

She met disaster.

Drawers had been emptied and flung across the room. Scents and powders and makeup splattered the floor and walls. Bed linens lay in a pile as if waiting to be laundered. Even to her inexperienced eye the room appeared to have been torn apart with no rhyme or reason. Just methodically undone.

Not quake damage, Felicia concluded, backing up until her legs collided with the living room sofa.

The image of the man with the duffle bag popped into her mind. She knew all of the tenants in the building. He wasn't one of them.

There was always a rash of burglaries and purse snatchings during quakes. Criminals and vandals took advantage of the confusion.

There was nothing written in stone that said a rapist, a thief, or a burglar had to be ugly. Good looks, a pleasant voice and a helpful attitude lured victims. Only a week ago she'd read of a woman who had been robbed by a stranger who had offered to help her change a flat tire.

Of course! The man had helped to open Lila's door so he could get a glimpse inside, to see if there was anything worth stealing. But Lila had slammed the door in both their faces, thereby saving herself from being—

Felicia's hand went to her throat. She had probably just missed being killed . . . or worse. If she had not stopped to help Lila, why, she might have caught the man in the act of destroying her bedroom.

Limbs feeling more leaden than ever, she picked up the phone and dialled 911. Clutching the receiver, she willed the panic out of her voice. "Hello. Police?"

"IT'S A MESS, ma'am, I'll grant you that," said the taller of the two officers. His name was Peterson. He moved from the bedroom to inspect the hall door, frame and lock. "There's some splintering, but it's not consistent. Looks like the door—"

"Does it matter how he got in? I've been vandalized," said Felicia. The shock had worn off, the adrenaline that had pumped into her was draining, leaving her irritated and exhausted. The officers had taken more than an hour to respond to her call. "Everything has been dumped out of my drawers. My closet has been—look at all my clothes!"

The short, stumpy officer named Unger lifted a piece of lace. To Felicia it seemed he fondled it. "You don't by any chance prance around in front of your windows wearing this stuff? Some guys would think it an invitation."

She yanked the lace teddy from his hand. "I didn't invite anyone to destroy my apartment. Naked or otherwise. And anyway, I've been out of town for a week. My mother died..."

The officers exchanged looks. Peterson said, "I'm sorry. Are you certain you locked the door before you left?"

"Yes."

He looked skeptical. "Begging your pardon, ma'am, but in your distress...I mean if you were called away suddenly—"

"I locked the door!"

"Okay," he conceded. "You locked it."

Officer Unger spoke. "I've got a teenager whose room looks like this all the time."

"Mine doesn't," Felicia shot back. "I'm neat."

"Really, miss, the quake could've done this—"

"It wasn't that strong a quake. Those drawers were yanked out and flung across the room. My bed was made. Now it's unmade. Somebody broke into my apartment! Why don't you believe me?"

"Is anything missing?"

She issued a deep sigh of resignation. "Not that I can tell. But aren't there weirdos out there with fetishes?" Felicia shivered. "Something might be missing."

The officers exchanged another one of their looks.

Felicia's gray eyes glistened with a building fury. "I'm the victim here. Stop acting like it's my fault this happened. Anyway, I think I know who did this."

Officer Peterson rocked on his heels. "Oh?"

"A man..."

"Someone you know well?" Officer Unger's innuendo was unmistakable. "You had a spat with your boyfriend?"

Felicia glowered at the policeman. "A man with broad shoulders. He had dark auburn hair. It was curly on the top, long on his neck. He was carrying a duffle bag. Blue, I think. He looked tough. He needed a shave. He had big hands," she added, recalling the size of his balled fists. "He was in the downstairs hall. I've never seen him before. I could sketch a good likeness though."

"A big-handed man with an underwear fetish."

Felicia's anger smoldered. "You think this is funny?"

Officer Peterson sighed. "No, ma'am. What I think is—you live in an old building that shakes like crazy when we get a one-point-zero on the Richter. You think this is bad, you ever been in a grocery store after a quake? You can't even walk the aisles for the debris."

"What's happening? Felicia, dear, are you okay?"

"Come in, Alphonse," said Felicia to her neighbor. The old gentleman always smelled of bay rum and clean starch. He was soft of voice and kind and Felicia liked him.

Close on his heels came Clare Epstein, a sweet septuagenarian with rounded face, bosom and hips. She looked like a little bundle of pink pudding. She'd never married and she had a crush on Alphonse.

Mildred Carstairs, Clare's live-in companion, the more domestic of the two, peeked past Clare's shoulder. Mildred was long, thin, and wore her hair rolled in what she called "rats," the style of the Forties. She loved big-band music and was just a bit too acerbic for Felicia's taste. But, considering the circumstances, Felicia was happy to see all three familiar faces. Perhaps they could help convince the officers that her apartment *had* been burglarized.

"All of you come on in. No need to hide out in the hall."

Mildred huffed. "I wasn't hiding."

"Neither was I," said Clare.

"Well," said Felicia. "Now that we're all here…did anyone, besides me, see a stranger in the building today?"

"I'll ask the questions," said Officer Peterson.

Felicia demurred with sweet-toned irony. "By all means, sir."

"Any of you folks have a problem during the tremor?" he asked. "Before? After?"

"The dishes fell off the counter," said Clare. "But that wouldn't have happened if Mildred had put them away like I told her."

"It wouldn't hurt you to do housework for a change. But no! You leave it all for me."

"Not now, girls," said Alphonse. "Felicia's upset. We were sorry to hear about your mother, Felicia."

Mildred elbowed her way across the room and put a bony arm around Felicia. "How was the funeral, dear? Did your mother look all right?"

"Mildred!" chastised Clare. "For heaven's sake."

"Don't take that tone with me, Clare. How the dead look the last time we ever lay eyes on them is important. If they look good in the casket—"

"Mother looked fine," Felicia said hurriedly over the lump forming in her throat.

"See?" admonished Mildred. "Now, forever more, Felicia will have wonderful recall of her mother before they closed the casket and—"

Wonderful recall was not Felicia's cup of tea at the moment. She was beginning to feel like an exhausted mouse being batted around for practice by a particularly nasty cat. "Listen, everyone. Someone broke into my apartment."

"Oh!" Clare clutched Alphonse's arm. "I need to sit down."

Mildred gave a snort. "Don't put on your frail act. You're strong as an ox."

"Leave me alone, Mildred, I'm older than you."

"We haven't seen any strangers in the building," said Alphonse. "We returned only moments ago. We saw the police car out front—"

"Clare always needs moral support when she goes to the bank," purred Mildred.

Clare gave Mildred a nasty look.

Officer Peterson eyed Felicia. "Let's get back to your boyfriend."

"Felicia doesn't have any boyfriends," put in Mildred.

"You wouldn't know that if you weren't such a nosey parker," said Clare.

"Excuse me," Felicia put in, close to tears. "But doesn't anybody care that my apartment has been vandalized? I could have been killed." A picture of herself lying in a casket flashed through her mind.

There would be no one to miss her, no one to say she'd looked fine.

"Of course we care," cooed Mildred.

"Now, Ms. Bennington," said the policeman. "The way I see it, no real harm has been done. It looks to us as if the quake made that mess, or at least, most of it. Your locks are flimsy, so that's not to say somebody didn't randomly take advantage of the door being jarred open. We'll file a report. If you have any more problems, just give us a call." He signaled his partner to leave.

The old folks parted to allow the officers through.

Framed in space they created was the auburn-haired man.

Felicia stared. "That's him!" she cried. "That's the man I was telling you about!"

Chapter Two

Felicia watched the man step into her living room. He walked as if he owned it. Or had been there before.

"What's the trouble?" he asked pleasantly.

Everyone stared at him. Seemingly undaunted, he smiled at Felicia.

He had a wonderful smile. It revealed well-kept teeth.

Don't pay any attention, Felicia told herself. Dracula had nice teeth too, until the urge for blood came over him.

"Look," she said. "He's still got the duffle bag. I told you it was blue!"

"Laundry," said the man. He smiled again, but the pupils of his eyes changed, and his posture altered, subtly indicating a wariness.

Officer Unger cocked an eyebrow. "You know Miss Bennington?" he asked, sounding for the first time as if bent on police business.

"Not personally. I've seen her name on the mailbox downstairs."

"You have too met me. You helped me open Lila's door not two hours ago."

"I don't believe we exchanged names."

Officer Peterson addressed Felicia. "This is the guy you think vandalized your apartment?"

"He was here. He just admitted it. He could have," she added lamely.

"A guy helps you and the first thing you do is accuse him of a crime?"

"Felicia is dreadfully independent," said Clare.

"Stay out of this, Clare, Please."

"Tragedy does not excuse sassiness," the older woman muttered.

"I don't understand why anyone would steal from Felicia," put in Mildred, glancing about the room. "Why, our things are so much nicer."

"Shh," said Alphonse.

"It wasn't like this man is saying," Felicia said to the policeman. "He disappeared really fast."

"Maybe he had to find a telephone booth, like Superman," said Clare, fluttering her lashes like bat wings. "He's cute."

"Do act your age, Clare," said Mildred. "All eighty years of it."

"Ted Bundy was cute, too," Felicia pointed out. "And they suspect he left a trail of dead women from Washington to Florida." To the police, she said, "Ask him what he's got in the duffle."

The man took a step back. "Now, hold on a minute—"

"Why don't you just empty the sack, mister?"

"I'm not dragging my underwear out in front of ladies."

"Aren't we shy?" Officer Unger grabbed the bag and dumped its contents. The man went rigid, observing the policeman from a still point that seemed unreachable.

The look on his face made Felicia drop her gaze to the pile of clothes. Male items. Socks. Undershorts, undershirts. Not a piece of silk or lace. She still couldn't let go. "Ask him what he's doing in this building."

"I live here."

Felicia gasped. "You don't!"

"Apartment five." He gestured to indicate the apartment across the hall from hers.

"Five is vacant!"

"Not since two o'clock this afternoon. Check with Cooper if you like."

"Who's Cooper?"

"He owns the building," said Alphonse.

"Such a nasty man," added Mildred. "We've had leaky faucets for over a month now, haven't we, Clare."

Clare's attention was fixed on the building's newest resident. Felicia imagined she could see the old woman's nose twitching with curiosity. The man accepted the veined, yet elegant hand Clare thrust at him. "It's so nice to meet you, Mr...?"

"Pritchard. Harry Pritchard, the Third."

"The Third? Oh, my," said Clare. "Well, we'll call you, Harry. Why don't you come down to the garden out back and have a drink? We always have just a short one before dinner. Settles the stomach, you know. And after all this excitement you need one, surely. Come along, Mildred. You, too Alphonse. Felicia, you poor dear. If you feel the need for company—"

Felicia shook her head.

Harry stepped aside as they trooped out. In passing, Alphonse thrust out his hand. Harry shook it.

Officer Peterson verified Harry Pritchard's identity via his driver's license; asked for and was shown a corroborating piece of identification, which caused him to murmur with the utmost respect "Just doing our job, sir." He tossed a parting "ma'am" in Felicia's direction. In the next instant he was hustling his protesting partner out of the apartment as if their lives depended upon the speed of their retreat.

Felicia found herself alone in her apartment with Harry Pritchard, the Third, new neighbor and positively still a stranger.

So what if he had just moved in? Even vandals had to live somewhere. Besides, his light-colored beard stubble gave him the look of a man toughened by the turmoil of life; one who had learned to look around all corners.

She took up a position of safety behind the kitchen counter and watched him kneel down, gingerly so, it seemed to her. He scooped up his clothes and shoved them deep into the duffle bag.

"Welcome to the neighborhood," he said, sarcasm thick on every word.

Felicia chewed the inside of her lip. "Well, I'm sorry. You should've introduced yourself downstairs."

"I was in a hurry. Besides, from the back you looked like a kid. And I had already met the old lady when I was moving some of my stuff in."

Like a kid. His reference to her lack of height, always a sore spot, irritated Felicia. Harry Pritchard strolled toward her bedroom. That didn't sit well with her, either.

"Stay out of there!"

"I agree, your place has been trashed, and not by the tremor." He stood just inside the bedroom, taking in the devastation. He nodded his head. "It took a lot of angry energy to create this mess." He glanced back at her. "Do you have a wealth of angry energy, Felicia?"

She stiffened. "You think I'd destroy my own bedroom and call the cops?"

"People have been known to do stranger things."

"I'm not strange."

"For attention, you know. Lonely and all that. But, even as he said it, Harry knew instinctively that Felicia had not created this chaos, nor had the earthquake. The earthquake had been little more than a tremor. Which meant that someone *had* entered her apartment. And that someone had a lot of hostility.

"You think I destroyed my own place just to get attention?"

"I was just making a supposition. Don't take it to heart." He would like to ask Felicia some questions, get a handle on who in her life might have acted out such anger, and warn her. But of course, she'd undoubtedly see that as suspect, too.

"Get out of my apartment."

He moved to the middle of the living room. "Is it true?" he asked, smiling.

Felicia eyed him as if he were about to pounce. "Is what true?"

"That you don't have a boyfriend."

"You eavesdropped?"

"The door was open." An understatement, he thought, but what the hell—

"Look, Harry Pritchard the Third, or whatever you call yourself, how about crossing the hall. That is, if you really live there."

He slid a hand into the pocket of his jeans—jeans that Felicia couldn't help but notice hugged his hips nicely. He displayed a key. "I do indeed live there. Living there is going to be interesting, I think."

"Don't count on us being friends, Mr. Pritchard."

"Oh, now, don't be so stiff-necked. I'm just plain, old Harry."

"To all of your friends?" Felicia mocked.

He laughed. "I'm Harry to my enemies, too."

Now she recognized the smile; it was à la Redford. The man no doubt had spent hours in front of his mirror perfecting it. "You're an actor, aren't you? Or trying to be."

"You mean you think I have that hungry look?"

"If you mean ghoulish, yes."

He pursed his lips. "Very funny. As it happens I've acted a bit in my day—in the streets, though. Where it counts."

"I suppose my line should be 'I want to hear all about it.'"

Harry shook his head. "Nope. At second glance I knew you were not a woman who looks for boredom."

"Would you please leave?"

"Has anyone ever told you that you have magnificent eyes?"

Felicia frowned. "I'm immune to flattery, especially from the likes of you."

"I'll leave my door open just in case you get frightened or just want to talk. I overheard about your mother, too. I'm sorry."

Pain flickered in Felicia's eyes. "I don't need sympathy from you."

Harry sighed. He hated vulnerability in women. He always noticed it and felt obliged to do something. He'd help old ladies cross streets or hold a baby while its mother rummaged for bus fare at the bottom of her purse. It wasn't too often he got thanked for his trouble then, either. Don't look for thanks, his mother always told him. Just put your good deeds into the universe. They'll come back to you. Harry shook his head. He obviously wasn't doing something right.

"When I left here," he said, "just before I met you downstairs, I noticed your door was ajar. I figured the quake did it and tried to close it. I think the hinge is bent."

"I appreciate your mentioning it," Felicia replied, standing pole straight. "I'll deal with it."

"I'm sure you will." At the threshold he turned back.

He looked down at his Adidas-clad feet for a heartbeat, then lifted his head and met Felicia's gaze again. "We are going to be friends. We have a lot in common. We're both pig-headed, narrow-minded and jump to conclusions. And on that note—" he shifted the duffle to his shoulder "—see you around... neighbor."

Lingering a moment longer, he smiled *the smile* as if it were a talisman.

"I almost forgot. When you accused me of being the vandal...well...you put two and two together and came up wrong, but that's okay. Anyone might have done it. But that business of comparing me to a convicted and executed killer..." He glowered and said, "I'd say you owe me an apology for that."

His rebuke lingered in the air but Felicia felt compelled to keep her mouth shut. He waited a moment in silence, then exited her apartment.

Slamming the door behind him was out of the question. The hinge *was* bent. Felicia forced the door closed, put on the chain and arranged a chair under the knob. Then she waded through the debris in the bedroom and stared at her image in the mirror.

Magnificent eyes.

He was just saying that.

Looked like a kid.

He'd said that, too.

"Brain always makes up for brawn," came Winifred Bennington's voice from deep in Felicia's memory.

"Oh, Mom . . ." she said, and let the tears come.

LILA STROKED Tweedledee's iridescent feathers as it pecked at a piece of banana she held in her palm. She had named the parakeets Tweedledee and Tweedledum. She couldn't tell them apart, so whichever one she stroked was always Tweedledee.

She had wanted a cat, but Sadie was allergic to cats. Lila wished now she had bought a cat. Then Sadie would be sneezing and her nose would be all stuffy. It would have served Sadie right for making the police come. Lila nodded her head emphatically then suddenly sensed the other woman's presence.

"You're angry with me, aren't you, Lila dear?"

"They went upstairs," Lila said, her voice flat.

Sadie affected a tone of insouciance. "So?"

"Don't take that attitude with me, Sadie." Agitated, Lila moved to the bird cage and gently placed the parakeet on the tiny swing. It ducked its head and began to clean the soft downy feathers beneath its wing. "I wish I had left you at the hospital, Sadie. I do. You always cause me trouble. And if Ernest finds out you're here..."

Sadie laughed. "Ernest, Smernest. Your son is a money-grubbing wimp. He doesn't want you. If he did, you think we'd be living here? In this dump? He just wants your money."

"But you insisted that I talk him into letting me live here," Lila said, feeling betrayed. "You said to tell him that this building was full of old folks and that I'd feel at ease here. That's what you said."

"If the rent hadn't been right, we wouldn't be here no matter how much you begged."

"I didn't beg," Lila said, mustering her dignity in the face of Sadie's accusations. "I just said what you told me to say. Anyway, I don't care if Ernest takes all my money. I just want my necklace back. We can't let anybody know we're looking for it, Sadie. We have to be careful."

Lila felt Sadie stroking her hair; Sadie's touch was always feather light, barely perceptible. Lila was obliged to stand very still or miss the sensation entirely.

"Oh, my dear, dear sweet," said Sadie. "Haven't I always looked after you? Remember how Papa used to make you work in the butcher shop? Didn't I do all your dirty work for you? Remember how you used to hate to go into the freezer or make sausage? Stuffing all those ropes and ropes of pork gut?"

Lila shivered. "I can't help it if I have a weak stomach. But, all the same, if Ernest finds out you're here..."

"He won't."

Lila moved away from the bird cage and curled up on the sofa. "He'll find out. I just know he will."

"Only if you tell him. And you know what would happen then, don't you? Right back to the hospital you'd go. He'd have you declared incompetent. Then we'd never find the necklace."

Tears welled up in Lila's eyes. "I hate that place. I hate it! They were so mean to me!"

"They were mean to me, too. Don't worry. We'll never have to go back. We're going to take care of each other."

Lila's eyelids fluttered. "You promise? You won't leave me?"

"I'll always be nearby," Sadie cooed.

"And, you're certain we'll find my necklace?"

"Of course we will. Percy gave it to that whore—"

Lila put her hands over her ears. "Sadie! I wish you wouldn't talk like that."

"What else would you call her? We followed Percy didn't we? Your dear, sweet husband. Didn't we climb the fire escape together and see them through the window. The slut didn't even bother to pull the drapes.

"Hugging and kissing and taking their clothes off. Percy was vulgar. I warned you about him, but would you listen? No. You just had to marry him. And how did he repay your devotion? By taking up with a woman of loose morals. He gave her your necklace."

Lila picked up a silver-framed photograph from the lamp table. In it she and Percy stood linked arm and arm. The opals were about her neck. Even as she gazed at the photo they seemed to come alive; milky white with patterns of shifting colors inside, sparkling with colors of wine. Eyestones, Mama had called them.

Papa had said that opals were bad luck.

But Lila knew better. They were magic, powerful. She traced the opals with a fingertip.

"It was my fault Percy took up with her. You know that, Sadie. I just couldn't be a good wife to him."

"But he didn't have to give your heirlooms away, did he? Was that right? He gave that woman Mama's necklace."

Lila sighed. "I do want my opals back. I just wish we could ask Percy—"

"Well, we can't. Percy's dead and that's that."

Lila put her head down on the sofa cushion and closed her eyes. "For the life of me, I just don't remember Percy getting dead."

Sadie's touch was light upon her forehead, hardly more than a waft of breeze. So gentle, Lila thought, so comforting.

"You don't have to remember, sweet dear. It was awfully like Papa's butcher shop. I remember it for you."

"I never did like the smell in the shop," Lila said. "It was like old copper, going all green."

"Yes, it was. Rest now."

"Are the police going to ask us questions about apartment six?"

"No, they've gone."

"What did you do up there, Sadie? Why did the police come?"

Sadie was silent. Her silence seemed sullen. Lila cringed. She couldn't bear it when her best friend was angry. "Sadie?"

"I'm here."

"You're certain no one saw you up there?" Lila asked, trying to make amends.

"Positive," said Sadie.

Lila's eyes flew open. "You're sounding smug, Sadie. I hate it when you sound like that. It always used to get me into so much trouble with Mama and Papa."

"You won't be in trouble with Mama or Papa ever again. They died years ago."

Lila returned her gaze on the opals in the picture. Sometimes she could stare at them so long she went into a trance, setting herself adrift. Like she was floating on a puffy white cloud. "And Percy's dead, too?"

"Percy is very dead."

"But before he died, he gave my necklace to . . . to that woman?"

"Of course he did. Where else could it be? Didn't we search the house from top to bottom? Just don't you worry, we'll find your opals."

Lila desperately wanted to believe Sadie and surrender to her optimism, but threads of doubt wove a pattern in her mind. "Sadie?"

"What, dearest."

"How long has Percy been dead?"

She felt Sadie withdraw her fingertips. "Oh, months and months."

"It seems like only yesterday."

"I know. It's a shame. The older we grow, the more faulty is memory."

Lila felt her entire body begin to go limp. She whimpered. "I don't like dead."

"I know you don't, sweet Lila, that's why I'm here."

A car squealed to a stop at the curb out front. A door slammed. Lila moved off the sofa to peer out between the drapes. She liked having windows facing

Catalina Street. She could observe all who came and went without being observed herself. Even when it was dark, like now, she could see. Light seemed to pour into the street from the laundromat across the way.

Lila gasped. Ernest. And, oh! He looked every inch his father's son. He had the same florid complexion, the same gait, the same huge belly. For a moment Lila even imagined he *was* Percy. She jerked away from that frightening thought.

"Sadie," she cried in panic. "You'll have to go. Ernest is here."

Chapter Three

Felicia surveyed the jumble and disorder that had been her neat and comfortable bedroom. Someone had entered her safe place. It was scary, unthinkable. It made her empty.

Someone unknown, a stranger, had handled her things. She felt she herself had been violated. That violation encroached on her grief and the aching sense of loneliness that so recently had threatened to overwhelm her.

By rote she vacuumed, dusted, swept, folded clothes and put fresh linen on the bed. The mindless activity helped.

Her small garden of potted plants had survived her absence, sitting in the three inches of water she'd left in the bathtub. What an odd twist of nature, she thought, that her plants had survived the week, while her mother had not.

She coaxed the floor-to-ceiling bedroom window open and propped it with a sawed-off broom handle. Back and forth she went, arranging the plants in their usual places on the rust-flecked fire escape.

The night air was mild, redolent with eucalyptus. The fragrance was stronger than usual. Crickets chirped in greenery. Perhaps, Felicia mused, tremors and quakes were nature's way of uncapping the scents and sounds of the universe.

Or, she thought, she was just more alert to sounds and scents and sights—more aware of being alive. Funerals, she supposed, had that effect. No doubt having one's home violated had something to do with it, too.

There were no lights in the backyard. The sodium-vapor lamps at the distant ends of the back alley were little more than glowing pinpricks of light, none of which filtered over the fence and into the backyard gloom. She was more aware of the darkness, too.

She glanced to her left. She shared the fire escape with apartment five. It seemed strange to see a patch of light pouring out of a bedroom window, twin to her own.

His bedroom.

She heard a noise, an alien sound. Her chest constricted, heart quickening.

An aftershock? she wondered. She put her hand out, touching the rough exterior masonry of the building. No, she felt no trembling beneath her fingertips.

It took several seconds for the sound to register. The fire escape's metal staircase, rattling.

Though once solidly grounded in concrete at its base, forty years of tremors had shaken it loose. It swayed and creaked with her weight every time she carried the garbage down. Now it swayed and creaked with another's weight.

The twin squares of light did not carry to the base of the stairs. The soft thud of footsteps rang out in the dark. Her mouth went dry.

"Who's there?"

Heavy breathing.

"I'm calling the police!"

A groan. "It's just me."

"Who?"

"Harry."

He came into the light, crawling up the steps on all fours, his muscular biceps and corded forearms taking most of his weight, his face bathed in sweat.

Her fright receded, but it took a minute for her to catch her breath. She watched Harry twist about and sit on the landing. The light shone on his face for a brief moment.

"What's wrong?" she asked, concerned. "Were you mugged? Are you hurt?"

He spoke through clenched teeth. "Hurting is the word for it."

"What happened?"

"Nothing much." He sighed with self-directed disgust. "I have a pair of bum knees. I was jogging—or trying to. They gave out on me."

Felicia's curiosity was aroused but she held it in check, imagining that he was suffering from some old high school or college football injuries. No, not football. Though he was well-built and strong looking, he did not have the height and breadth one associated with football players.

Having so little of it herself, height was a thing Felicia noticed. Tall men tended to view her as cute and cuddly, a caricature of a woman. She'd been rebelling against that image since fifth grade.

A deep-down, internal dignity prevented her from using artificial means to create an image of height. She couldn't countenance spiked heels or hairstyles that added inches. No matter how attractive the man, she refused to date him if he towered above her. Eventually he'd start calling her Short Stuff, or Peanut, or some such endearment that got her dander up. End of relationship.

Looking at Harry with a measuring eye she decided she would probably come up to his chin—well within her criteria. But of course, she had a whole list of other expectations, and Harry Pritchard was not the man to fill any of them.

He was staring at her, she realized, surfacing suddenly from her thoughts. She felt her face grow warm. She'd been so rude to him earlier, he probably was thinking she was a harridan and uncaring.

"I have some aspirin . . ." she volunteered, noticing that he was massaging his knees with such pressure that his knuckles had turned white. His breathing was still a bit ragged.

"I'm all right now, but thanks anyway."

He had sensed Felicia was taking his measure by some standard of her own and he had allowed the process to go on undisturbed.

It was a trick he had learned early as a rookie cop. He figured he could tell where he stood with someone if he let them make up their own mind. Most people gave off sharp clues to what their impression was. He wondered what Felicia had decided about him.

"Well, if you're sure you're all right . . ." she said, moving back from neutral ground into the patch of light she considered her own.

"Right as rain," he said, turning to study the self-conscious smile she gave him. "I heard you scurrying about putting your place back together. Did you find anything missing?"

"No, nothing."

He raised a copper-colored eyebrow. "An odd bit of work, destroying your bedroom like that."

"I don't want to think about it."

"Are you scared?"

"I'm a little on edge." But more than that, Felicia recognized she was on emotional overload. Continuing to converse with Harry was straining her internal resources further. She expelled a barely perceptible sigh. "If you'll excuse me . . ."

"Sure, sleep tight. Bang on the wall or floor if you hear anything go bump in the night you want checked out."

She was surprised by the real concern she heard in his voice. "Yes, okay, I will."

She turned and stepped over the low windowsill.

When Harry had first encountered her in the downstairs hall, he'd thought her a child. She wasn't. Small though she might be, she was to his eye, perfectly proportioned. He had the idea that his hands could span her waist. He dwelt on that thought a moment.

He shifted his weight, preparing to stand. Pain shot through his knees. He winced. Damn! He'd be sleeping with ice bags tonight.

The far side of the fire escape dimmed as Felicia pulled her drapes. Only a sliver of light remained. Harry waited until that sliver of light disappeared, too. Then, jaw clenched, he pulled himself to his feet.

LATER, NEAR MIDNIGHT, as Felicia was lying in bed with the dark around her, she realized, against all odds she felt safe.

An acute sensation of loneliness was still lodged in the very depth of her soul. Yet...

She felt comforted and reassured by Harry Pritchard's presence next door.

How odd, she thought. Because with his bad knees he didn't appear likely to be able to protect himself, much less her. In her mind's eye she saw his thick and sinewy arms, recalled the tense, predatory impression that had emanated from him the moment she'd accused him of vandalism. Yet now he was at ease with her, and with the situation. The man next door, she mused, was not easily categorized.

At the moment she was too weary to sort him out. But he was right about one thing. She did owe him an apology.

AN INSISTENT KNOCK pulled Felicia out of bed and summoned her to the door. She removed the chair. The door sprang open, straining against the length of security chain.

"Open up, Felicia. It's me, Zelda."

"I'm trying to, but this door—" She pressed her shoulder against it, held it closed, and slid the chain out of its track. The bent hinge popped loose, the door jerked open again and dangled at an angle.

Zelda strolled across the threshold. "The quake did in your door, eh? I got a cracked window."

Felicia ran hands through her dark cap of hair. Sassoon short, most of it fell into place. "It did in more than my door. What're you doing here so early?"

Zelda cocked her head. "I was anxious about you. I'm your best friend. We've known each other for five years. Am I not the colleague who oversaw the placing of every single flower on your award-winning float in the Rose Parade? Is that any way to greet a friend who worries about you? I'm here to see how the funeral went, to hold your hand, offer sympathy. Have you cried yet?''

"I've cried. I'm cried out."

Zelda looked relieved. Felicia gave a small laugh, then closed her eyes a moment. It felt good to laugh. "You're transparent as all get out, Zelda."

"My horoscope said this morning was going to be interesting, but I have to be cautious in the afternoon, stay home, you know. You're the only interesting person I know, so here I am. Besides, I figured you'd be needing your car keys." She held them out to Felicia. "I only had time to go by and start it once."

"Once? Zelda, you promised . . ."

"It wasn't in my chart."

"Oh, Zelda. Why do you let something as silly as astrology rule your life?"

Zelda huffed. "If it's good enough for Nancy Reagan, it's good enough for me. This way, I know what days to stay home, what days to be careful, when to accept a date—"

"—everytime you're asked."

Zelda laughed. "True, but my chart tells me whether to entertain at home or go out. So there. You'll see. I'm having Thea do your astrological chart for your birthday."

"No."

"You'd refuse my birthday gift to you? Hurt my feelings? Just like that. Thea's a little bit psychic, too."

"A psychic is just what I need."

"To contact your mother?" Zelda said, all hope.

"To tell me who trashed my apartment while I was gone."

"What!" Zelda dropped to the sofa. "You were robbed?"

"Just vandalized.

"Just! Who would do such a thing? Your stuff is all so...so—"

"Shabby but comfortable?"

"I mean, what do you keep here that would interest anybody? Except your sketches—"

Color drained from Felicia's face. "Oh! I didn't—" She raced to the bedroom, jerked up the floor-dragging linen bedspread and looked beneath the bed. The huge brown portfolio was there. She put it atop the bed, opened it and skimmed through her sketches of float designs, of whimsical animals, comic strip characters, blueprints and schematics detailing the view of floats from front, back, side and top. Nothing had been tampered with.

She felt an immense relief, but it took a moment for her thudding heart to subside to normal.

The sketches were ready to be used for a portrait rendering for the Tournament Association's approval and the parade brochure. Had they been damaged, she would've had to redo them. A loss of weeks.

"Everything is okay."

Zelda stood on the threshold. "I can't imagine those weren't the first things you checked."

"A lot was going on. I was thinking about Mom, the police were here..." Felicia closed the portfolio. "You know where everything is, Zelda—please, go make coffee."

"I thought we might walk over to Green Street for breakfast. They have a new coffee shop, the Bagel. I hear it's wonderful."

Felicia's expression filled with regret. "Not today, okay? I really need to just hang around here, get my bearings." She disappeared into the bathroom and gave herself over to the ritual of brushing her teeth. Then she dressed quickly in an old skirt and blouse from deep in her closet.

She had folded much of her wardrobe in a corner—items she would launder before wearing again. That was the only way she could think of to exorcise the essence, the presence, of whoever had touched them.

When she joined her friend, Zelda was staring into the fridge. "Say, Felicia, I didn't know you had an interest in science."

"I don't."

"Really? Everything in your fridge but this—" she held up a carton of English muffins "—is growing penicillin."

Felicia winced. "I didn't have time to clear things out before I left."

Zelda popped the muffins into the toaster, then she began heaping sugar into her coffee.

"I thought you were off sugar," Felicia said.

"I was, but the ten pounds I gave up are lonesome for me." She took a sip of coffee and grinned happily. "I'll never make it as a California girl anyway. Forget the blond hair and legs up to here, I can't abide bean sprouts, sushi, or herb teas. There's just something about being Texan that's genetic."

Felicia smiled. Zelda was every bit as attractive as her description of a California girl. She just wasn't consistent with it. She had green eyes, clear skin that tanned easily and natural brown hair. But she was forever experimenting with makeup and hair color. At the moment Zelda was a redhead with silver, frosted highlights.

"Like how, genetic?"

"Like the craving for thick steaks, enchiladas, refried beans, cold beer, angel food cake with white fudge icing, coffee with sugar."

"Oil wells?"

"Don't mention oil. Royalties are way down. Daddy said I may even have to go on a budget."

"Or show up to work every day so your paycheck isn't docked?"

"Don't make jokes. I'll need your birth certificate."

"Somehow that doesn't compute."

"To have your astro chart done, silly. Thea needs to know the date and time of birth. She has to plot your horoscope according to the planet's position at the exact moment you were born."

Felicia leaned on the kitchen counter. "I can't talk you out of this?"

"Nope. See, if you had a chart, you would've known that there might be a tragedy in your life—"

"I did know. Mom had been ill for months—"

"But you weren't prepared. Not really for her dying. And you would've been warned against vandalism. You could've protected yourself."

"It's hard to prepare for the death of one's last living relative on the face of the earth."

"You're feeling sorry for yourself?"

"I guess I am," Felicia said. Then she added, "I don't even know where my birth certificate is," hoping that would put an end to Zelda's insistence. "Come to think of it, I don't recall ever seeing it."

"Oh, c'mon. What about when you got your driver's license?"

"Mom took me. She had it, I guess."

A look of empathy swept across Zelda's features. "These are things you'll have to keep up for yourself, now. You're always saying you feel incomplete. Maybe if your birth certificate were in hand, you'd feel you have your own special place in the universe."

Felicia sipped her coffee. "If I have a special place in the universe, I wish someone would point it out to me."

"Thea will."

Felicia smiled and propped her chin into her palm. "I walked into that one."

"You did. Now, where would your birth certificate be? Let's hunt it up."

Felicia indicated one of the as yet unpacked suitcases. "I dumped everything out of Mom's writing table into one of those. There was so little..."

"Don't go maudlin, Felicia. I'll start cry—" Zelda stopped mid-word, her gaze sweeping beyond Felicia's shoulder. "You have company," she said, adding sotto voce, "Boy, do you have company."

Felicia twisted around on the breakfast stool.

"Morning, neighbor," said Harry. "I could smell that coffee all the way across the hall." This morning he wore jeans and a gray sweatshirt with the sleeves cut out. Auburn hair curled over the cusp of the stretched neckline. The hair on his head was shower damp and he had shaved. It made him appear much more presentable. A cup dangled from his fingers.

"Still eavesdropping, I see," said Felicia. "Somebody ought to teach you manners."

"My-oh-my," said Zelda, her voice heavy with Texas drawl. "Let me be that somebody."

Harry laughed.

Felicia frowned. "Zelda Graham, meet my new neighbor, Harry Pritchard."

Zelda undulated across the room and took Harry's cup. "Cream and sugar?"

"Black." He looked at Felicia. "You don't mind? I didn't have time to—"

Felicia didn't know whether she minded or not, but to refuse would've been mean-spirited. She realized she did not want Harry to think her either mean or rude. "It's okay. I know how it is, just getting settled."

He looked around. "You've got things in tip-top shape. Looks nice."

"Thank you."

Zelda placed his cup on the counter. After a moment's hesitation, Harry moved to pick it up. Zelda smiled. "Sit down. We're just having English muffins..."

Harry sat, elbow to elbow with Felicia, suddenly very much aware of her, the texture and color of her skin, creamy and untanned. "Just coffee will do. Unless..." He grinned lazily and gazed at Felicia. "You're ready to offer that apology?"

There was no hint of condescension in his expression. "Consider it offered," she said. He smelled heady and masculine. His hands cradled the coffee cup. She wondered what it would be like to be held by him.

On the opposite side of the counter, Zelda looked from one of them to the other. Felicia's expression had gone tense, Harry's cautious. "Something tells me I'm going to have to carry the conversation here."

"It's early in the morning for me," said Harry.

"Me, too," said Felicia.

"Well, all right, why don't I bore both of you with my life story."

"Zelda..." Felicia warned.

"Okay. We'll pass on that. Harry, tell us all about you."

He cleared his throat. "Nothing to tell. I'm a late bloomer, finishing up law school over at UCLA."

Zelda's green eyes sparkled. "Promising. Very promising. And what were you before you began to bloom, like in the bud stage?"

He sighed. This would do it. "A cop."

Felicia became alert. "So that's why the police began bowing and scraping the moment they checked your I.D."

"I wouldn't say they bowed and scraped."

Zelda's eyebrows shot up. "Why aren't you a cop now?"

"Ah, well...I got hit in the knees."

Felicia butted in. "Hit?"

"Right. As in shot."

"Ooo," cooed Zelda. "I want to hear all the gory details. Were you on a case? Did we read about it in the paper?"

"I doubt it," he said stiffly. It wasn't a moment he liked to recall.

"But it must've been recently," Felicia said, looking at him, recalling their conversation on the fire escape last night.

"No... I've had knee replacements."

"Oh. I'm sorry."

"Nothing to be sorry about," he said, trying to be blasé. "You get a choice—ceramic, metal, or plastic."

"But who shot you?" Zelda asked. "Were you in a gun battle?"

"Ahh, not exactly. A woman shot me," he said, looking as if he felt, by admitting that, he was revealing a treacherous vein of weakness in his nature.

Zelda was almost speechless. "A woman shot a gorgeous creature like you? Hang her by her toes!"

He laughed self-consciously, more aware than ever of Felicia since she was remaining silent. He moved off the stool. "Thanks for the coffee. My treat next time."

It was then that Felicia noticed his unusual eyes. They were pale amber gold, just like the rest of him. "Sure."

"I'll come over later to replace that bent door hinge for you."

"Oh, no," she said too quickly. "Cooper'll have someone over here today, I'm sure." Shot, she was thinking. How awful.

He smiled. "He does. Me. I get a bit off the rent for agreeing to take care of odds and ends of maintenance. Saves him a trip over."

He walked out and across the hall to his own apartment.

Felicia turned to Zelda. "All the gory details? Where's your sense of... of..."

"I've never met anybody who's been shot before. I mean you hear about it, read about it. Anyway, he doesn't seem any worse for it. I suppose you're calling dibs on him."

Felicia bristled. "I suppose I am not."

"He hardly gave me a glance. He's interested in you."

"Zelda—go home."

"Gee, you sure are touchy. Can't we find your birth certificate first?"

"If that's what will get you out of here," Felicia said, hauling one of her suitcases over to the sofa. "Then I've laundry to do and grocery shopping. And I've got to go all the way across town to Von's to do it."

"Speaking of doing, I've got a side job painting an Indian rug design on a porch over in the Arroyo Seco area. Pay's good. Wanna help?"

"When? Before I commit to anything I have to check out how much things have backed up over at the float barns this week."

"Next Saturday?"

"Depending upon what your horoscope says?"

"That's not nice, Felicia. Besides, it already says next Saturday will be a day of financial gain. The lady is gonna pay cash."

Felicia snapped the suitcase open and stared down at the jumble of papers and photos within. "Okay," she agreed absently. "I suppose I can manage the time Saturday."

Chapter Four

They were sitting on the floor with the suitcase contents spread out. The musty smell of old paper hung in the air.

"Ohh, weren't you a cute thing. Look at this picture, Felicia. How old were you then?"

"Four or five. I don't remember. Skip the photos for now, okay?"

Zelda sighed. "You really make it hard for a friend to be compassionate."

A look of pain crossed Felicia's features. "I don't mean to, but I've just survived the worst week of my life. Things seem so different..." She set aside several envelopes of canceled checks. Damn! I have to keep all the financial stuff of Mom's. Did you know that even after a person dies, you still have to file a tax return for them?"

"That's awful. What would the IRS do if you don't? Hold the body hostage?"

"That's a sick joke."

"It's called black humor, and it did make you smile. Ah, here we are." Zelda shook the contents of a brown envelope out into her lap. "Here's your parent's marriage certificate. Boy, look at all that ornate gilt scrolling. I wonder if that's how they look now? Not that it matters. I'd be happy with a marriage certificate written on the back of an envelope.''

In spite of the way she was feeling, Felicia laughed. "You wouldn't. Not really."

"Yes, I would! Adam. You never told me your Dad's name was Adam. Here's his death certificate . . ." Zelda looked up. Felicia was studying an old sepia-colored photo of her parents, her eyes glinting with threatening tears. "Oh, say. Maybe we ought to do this another time. Your birthday's not for another few weeks."

Felicia held up a photo. "Look at this. It's a picture of Dad and Mom when she was pregnant with me."

"What do you know! The earliest known snapshot of Felicia Marie Bennington."

"I think I'll have it framed in silver."

Zelda pulled a face. "Don't do that to your mother, Felicia. No woman likes to be remembered when she's all out of shape. My mother has destroyed every picture of herself that shows her weighing over a hundred and ten pounds. Aha! Here's your birth certificate." She smoothed it out.

"Good. Or maybe, bad. Zelda, I'm not sure I want to have an astrology chart done. Can't you think of anything else that would appeal?"

"Gifts are from the heart. My heart is New Age and astrology with a little psychic awareness thrown in. Anyway, I really want to do this for you. You'll be surprised how accurate an astrology reading can be."

"I'm not much for surprises, but, okay. I give up. Take it and go. I can sort out the rest of this later and turn what I have to over to an accountant and be done with it."

Zelda was reading Felicia's birth certificate, fascinated. "No wonder you're so small, you only weighed four pounds, one ounce when you were born. Gee, you never told me you were a twin."

Felicia did a double take. "I'm not."

Zelda held out the creased certificate. "See for yourself. Look at number five. Where it asked twin or triplet? The doctor wrote in 'yes—twin.'"

"But that's impossible. Mother would've told me. Or Dad. They wouldn't have kept something like that to themselves. What would be the point?"

"Well, it's your birth certificate. It has your name on it. Look at order of birth. You were born second."

Felicia felt goose bumps erupt on her arms. "But it just can't be. I mean all these years, I've felt something...incomplete...Mom knew that. She would've—" Felicia stopped her musings and just sat there, cross-legged, staring into space.

Zelda sorted quickly through the papers in her lap. She found what she was looking for and read it aloud. "Your twin was a boy. They named him Thomas Adam. He weighed three pounds, fourteen ounces. A live birth...uh-oh."

"What?" Felicia jerked. "What is it?"

"Where it says 'Supplementary data below are not part of the legal certificate. Question B asks about congenital malformation."

"Let me see that." Felicia read the tiny, impossible print. Congenital malformations? Yes, was scrawled in the blank. Her chest constricted. "That's why Mom and Dad never said anything. The poor thing. They must've felt awful. Can you believe it? I had a twin brother. Amazing. Still, they could've said something."

"I don't know. My aunt Evelyn had a stillborn baby years and years ago. It's a painful topic for her to this day. No one in the family dares to bring it up."

"Thomas Adam," Felicia mused softly. "I wonder how long he lived."

Zelda gathered together the papers in her lap and set them aside. "You'll be able to tell from his death certificate when you find it. Look, Felicia, I think I'll be going now. I'll drop by Thea's so she can get started on your chart. Unless you want to talk or something."

"Thanks, no. I have errands to run and clothes to wash." And I need time alone, she thought, time to absorb the fact that I have a brother.

"Now that you know twins run in your family," Zelda said mischievously, "you better keep it in mind when you get around to having babies yourself."

"I have to get around to having a husband first," Felicia replied dryly. "And that's not in the cards."

"Might be in the stars, though," Zelda said, making for the exit. She stood there for a second and stared at Harry's door. "Who knows? He might even be in the apartment next door."

Felicia laughed. "That is so far-fetched it doesn't even require an answer."

Zelda shook her head. "My dear, dear friend, I'm going to ask Thea to put a rush on your chart. You need it!"

"What I need is to get this door repaired." She saw Zelda out and made a futile attempt to close and latch the heavy door. It kept tilting out of her grasp.

Exasperated, she propped it open against the wall. Until Harry Pritchard came to repair the darn thing she was going to be tied to the apartment—which meant she'd have to reschedule her errands. She hesitated for only a moment, then crossed the hall to his apartment and rapped hard on the door.

No answer. Damn.

She went back through the apartment and out onto the fire escape and tapped on his window. "Harry?"

"He's not home, Felicia."

She spun about and looked down into the yard. Alphonse was there, leaning on a hoe. A frustrated farmer, he tended his tomato and cucumber plants among the flowers and shrubs planted by Mildred and Clare.

"He said he was going to repair my door."

"He's gone off to the hardware store to get parts and things. How're you feeling today?"

"Better, I'm getting back to normal, thanks."

Alphonse nodded, took a swipe at his sweat-streaked face with a snowy-white handkerchief and returned to his gardening.

Felicia gazed up at the sky. It was a lovely morning. One of those clear, sunny days sans smog that reminded native and non-native Californians alike why the most populated state in the country was just that. She sat on the fire escape steps, tucked her skirt modestly about her knees, closed her eyes and held her face up to the sun.

Dear God, but she missed her mother.

Soberly she reflected on her situation. She had a roof over her head, a job she loved, a best friend—and once she'd had a twin brother.

Unbelievable. Over the years she'd often felt at loose ends with the world. She'd put the feeling down to an unnamed yearning. But for what? Or why? Perhaps she had always yearned for her other self, her twin.

It did hurt that her mother had not mentioned she'd been a twin. She and her mother had been close, especially after her dad had died. Felicia exhaled. She'd never know why now.

The sun rose higher. A breeze swept into the San Gabriel Valley from the slopes of Mount Wilson. It brushed her cheeks and caught at the hem of her skirt.

Felicia didn't notice. In her mind, she was reflecting on the good times she'd had with her mother.

After Felicia had begun getting work as a float designer she had not been able to get home between Thanksgiving and New Year's. November and December were the hectic, chaotic months when last-minute details had to be worked out. But after the parade on New Year's Day, Felicia always managed at least a few days home.

She and her mom would tuck themselves into her mom's great old bed, sip frothy mugs of hot chocolate and talk the night away. Her mom had not seemed to hold anything back. She had been joyful, delighted with her daughter and all Felicia accomplished.

Felicia realized now it had never been her mother's way to burden others with her sorrows. She had not even told Felicia how ill she was until the signs were too obvious to miss.

Felicia opened her eyes, gazed for a moment at the sky and offered up a prayer for her father and mother; together now for all time. And in a corner of her heart, Felicia made room for the brother she had never known. She might still suffer those odd pangs of distance and loneliness, but now she knew why. She could go on with her life. Her parents, she knew, would still be keeping an eye on her.

A soft cough brought Felicia back to awareness of the sun, the fire escape, the gentle breeze.

Harry Pritchard was sitting on his windowsill, his arms resting on his knees. The sunlight gave his arms a look of sculpted and burnished gold. Felicia felt her heart speed up.

"You seemed so thoroughly engrossed in your daydream," he said. "I hated to disturb you."

"I wasn't daydreaming. I was..." She shook her head and wondered how long he'd been sitting there watching her.

"Go on," he encouraged, "say what you were going to say."

"What were you thinking about while you were watching me?" she countered.

For a moment his eyes narrowed. "The truth or something flippant?"

"Whichever you prefer."

"You had a wounded look on your face. Then you sort of smiled."

For a moment Felicia was nonplussed, surprised that he was so discerning—and honest. A bit self-consciously she said, "I was saying good journey and goodbye to my mom. I think I truly believe in Heaven now. Before I wasn't sure."

"I believe in Heaven," said Harry.

"You don't seem the type."

"I am. I believe in Hell, too."

The tiniest of smiles lifted the corner of Felicia's mouth. "That's more the type I had you pegged for."

Harry grinned. He'd been thinking he wouldn't mind raising a little hell with her. But he pushed such thoughts away. She was grieving for her mother. He'd respect that.

"I got the parts for your door and since I noticed it's hanging open..." But now he was noticing how the sun glinted off her hair and skin. She was free of make-up. He silently noted her natural attractiveness. For the first time in a long while he found himself profoundly interested in a woman. He was intrigued and charmed by her.

Her senses were taking him in, feeding ideas and thoughts into her mind. Man-woman thoughts that had no place in her life at the moment. She shifted her eyes away from him and smoothed her skirt. "If you can fix it now, I'd appreciate it. I've a half dozen errands to run."

He nodded agreement and two minutes later he was in her living room, removing the bent and useless door hinges.

Felicia stood in the middle of the room, staring at the floor with dismay. Not thirty minutes earlier photographs and papers had been haphazardly spread out everywhere. Now they were stacked tidily in the open suitcase on the sofa. She gazed at Harry. "Did you come in here and pick up all this stuff?"

"What stuff?"

"I had all my mother's papers out. Now they've been put away. Zelda and I were going through them."

"Maybe she—"

"No, I saw her out. And I left them scattered on the floor when I went looking for you—"

"Me?"

"To find out when you were going to fix the door. You weren't in so I decided to wait on the fire escape.

But somebody has been in my apartment again. This time they straightened it up!"

Harry laughed. "That's a new one."

"It's not funny."

"You probably did it yourself without thinking. You were in another world out there on the fire escape."

"I guess I know what I do, and when I do it."

The vexation in her tone made Harry look at her again. Her eyes were as gray as rain. Her dark brows were set off by a clear, fair complexion in a narrow oval face that appeared more suited to a sweet pixie smile than the look of frightened puzzlement she was displaying now.

He fought an urge to put a comforting arm around her. They were still too nearly strangers.

"Maybe Clare or Mildred came up here," he suggested reassuringly. "I fixed that leaky faucet for them before I went to the hardware store. They were talking about you, something about fixing you a covered dish or having you down to dinner." He turned back to installing the new hinges on her door.

"Mildred is the likely candidate," Felicia said. "She can spot a dustball at thirty paces. I'll go down and ask her." She brushed past Harry on her way out and turned back to add, "Don't let anyone in."

He saluted with the screwdriver. "Right. I shall guard the portals of your ivory tower with life and limb—well, maybe not limb. Too painful."

"If you went on stage with a line like that—they'd throw tomatoes."

"I'll take tomatoes over bullets any day of the week." He openly watched the graceful and lissome way she moved down the stairs. Inwardly he groaned.

Careful, Harry, old son, he warned himself. Such thoughts often lead to trouble.

Clare answered the door on the first knock. "Felicia, dear. Welcome. Mildred and I were just—"

"Did either of you come up to see me this morning?"

"Why, no. We haven't yet agreed on what to prepare—"

"I don't see what's to agree on," said Mildred. "I'm doing the cooking. It's my choice."

"I left my door open while I was outside and I think someone came in."

"Again? Did they steal something?" Clare pulled Felicia into the apartment and closed the door with a thud.

"No, this time whoever it was straightened up my living room."

"How thoughtful," said Mildred, sounding puzzled. "But it wasn't either of us. Anyway, it would never be Clare. She doesn't know one end of a broom from the other."

"I most certainly do. I'm just not into brooms."

"It couldn't have been Alphonse," Felicia said, trying to keep the old ladies on track. "He was out back while I was. I'll check with Lila."

The two old women exchanged looks. "Perhaps you shouldn't disturb her just now, Felicia," said Clare. "Ernest was here last night, and again this morning. You know how he upsets Lila. She's frightened of him."

"She's frightened of everybody," snorted Mildred.

Clare fixed Mildred with a stern eye. "Draw your horns in, Mildred. How would you feel if your son was looking over your shoulder all the time, just waiting for you to make one false move so he could stick you in a nursing home and forget about you?''

Mildred rolled her eyes. ''That's pure conjecture on your part. You're always making up stories to suit your whims. Anyway, the point is moot. I don't have any children. However, unlike you, it wasn't for lack of opportunity.''

Clare's long patrician nose quivered. ''Felicia does not want to hear you brag about your sex life. It's ancient history.''

Felicia angled toward the exit. ''Thanks, anyway. Harry must be nearly through repairing my door. I'd better get back.''

''Of course, dear. Anytime. And, we'll let you know when to come to tea. We'll have it in the garden.''

''That would be nice.''

Once in the hall, Felicia eyed Lila's door. The poor old thing couldn't get half a dozen steps from her apartment without going into a panic. It couldn't have been Lila, she decided as she trudged back upstairs.

''Any luck?'' Harry asked.

''No.''

''Well . . .''

Felicia reheated the coffee and reached for a cup. Reached.

Her hand stopped in midair.

''Someone *was* here!'' she shouted.

''I'm not disputing you,'' Harry said, thinking she was on the attack again.

Felicia turned. ''Look. Someone washed out my cups and put them away.'' She opened the cupboard and checked. ''They even washed the one you came over here with and put that one away, too. Somebody did this, damn it.''

"Maybe your friend."

"Not Zelda. I told you."

"Felicia...I've been thinking. My dad was killed in Korea. An incident in the demilitarized zone, the Army said. My mom was a basket case for weeks after she got the call. She forgot things...she misplaced things. She even misplaced the car once. Left it at the grocery store and came home on the bus. I was in school when she did it. It took two days of quizzing before she finally recalled that she'd even gone shopping." His voice was firm.

"But, I'm sure...I've been upset, but I haven't lost my mind. And, I'm certain..." But now she wasn't.

Harry lined the door up with its new hinges and tapped in the pintles. He swung the door closed, opened it and closed it again. "There you are. Good as new."

Felicia poured coffee. She offered Harry a cup. He accepted.

"You were a policeman. Tell me what kind of a person would break into somebody's apartment and clean it up?"

He smiled *the smile* and merely shook his head.

"All right. Maybe I did straighten things up without remembering I did it. But before you leave, I do remember that I owe you an apology. I was too embarrassed to say much in front of Zelda this morning. I was scared yesterday and, I guess I overreacted."

"That's it? That's your entire apology?"

She was taken aback. "What were you expecting?"

"Oh, something a little more effusive. Like...what about a picnic under the stars up in Arrowhead?" he said on impulse.

He was teasing. He had to be. "No, thanks." She smiled to soften her answer.

"Barbecue at Tony Roma's?"

Felicia shook her head.

"I could take you home to meet my mother and if she approves—"

"Aren't you ever serious!"

"I just can't win. Only last week I was told to loosen up." He sipped the coffee. "I wouldn't take advantage of you, if that's what's worrying you."

"I wouldn't allow you to take advantage of me."

"I'm a good listener."

"You're a good talker, too. It's just I'm not dating right now."

"Ah. One of those."

Felicia stiffened. He'd said it jokingly, but there was an edge in his voice she couldn't miss. "What do you mean? Oh, one of those?"

"Women. Under thirty they're interested in themselves and their careers and getting one up on the corporate ladder. Over thirty, they start worrying about the biological clock ticking down. Either way, a man is in trouble. He gets tossed aside by the ladder climber, and hog-tied by—"

"You're divorced aren't you?"

Harry sighed. "A cop's wife has a hard lot. Mine left me for an insurance salesman. Nice safe job. No worrying. He's home every night 6:00 p.m. on the dot."

"Children?"

"No. She saved her figure for the insurance salesman."

His smile was back but now he looked a little sheepish. Felicia laughed. "Are you trying to make me think you don't have much luck with women?"

"It's true. No luck at all, even on the job." He tapped his knee. "I was on a narc takedown. We busted into a house. There was a woman there. The guy we were after grabbed her to use her as a shield. But before he could slide behind her, my partner grabbed him. He wrestled him down and cuffed him. Then the woman reached under the bed as calmly as you please and pulled out a sawed-off shotgun. She said we were hurting her man." He smiled ruefully.

"That's awful."

"I was in the hospital for twelve weeks. Never did draw a pretty nurse."

Felicia nodded. The teasing tone was back in his voice. "I see. And how many times have you used that tale to get a date?"

"You think I made all that up?"

"Thanks for fixing my door."

"Sure." He gathered up his tools. "If you see any little green men about, washing dishes or dusting, just give me a yell. I might want to hire them myself."

Felicia accepted the jibe with a modicum of restraint. "Thanks to you," she intoned sweetly, "I can now secure my door against all men—green or otherwise."

"I get it," Harry said glumly. He had hoped for a chance to talk to her a little longer. "Beneath that innocent sweet facade of yours is a savage lusting animal burning with passion. I've treated you too nicely."

Laughing at his teasing tone, Felicia pushed him out into the hall.

The door closed and Harry heard the latch click and heard the security chain slide into place.

He had managed to pierce her grief and sense of reserve. He had even made her laugh. It was a start.

Felicia Bennington oozed the kind of sensuality men dreamed about. It was all the more striking because she appeared not to be aware of it.

On the other hand, he'd never before met a woman who was not aware of her sensuality. And if she were aware she could use it to tie a man in knots. That was trouble he didn't need.

From the apartments below came the sound of music, an old 1940s tune, "Shoo-Shoo Baby." He listened a moment, then whistled the melody as he made himself a potted meat sandwich. He'd only been in the apartment a day and a half. Already the place was a disaster. Whoever had cleaned up Felicia's apartment obviously hadn't visited him.

A well-used rowing machine filled the space in front of the sofa. He looked from it to the stack of law books on the card table that served as his desk. Leg therapy first, he decided. He need to get in shape.

He finished off the potted meat and washed it down with a swig of cola.

The tempo of the music coming from downstairs picked up with "GI Jive." Harry felt the rhythm in his bones. He smiled.

The forces that ruled his life were no longer vindictive. He was sure of it.

Chapter Five

He had spoken too soon. The forces that ruled his life were still vindictive. The force he faced at the moment was law professor Fred Lawson.

Lawson was bald, thin to the point of emaciation and wore tweed jackets with leather elbow patches. He had a reputation for offering private tutoring to his female students, all of whom found excuses to avoid a second session with him.

It was also rumored he skimmed student papers for article ideas which he then published under his own name. Harry had noticed that academic politics was often as underhanded and dirty as crime in the street.

What Harry disliked most about the professor was that he affected a pipe. If Lawson would light the damned thing once in a while, he could've tolerated the man. But Lawson just sucked air through the stem. The sound grated on Harry's nerves.

"I called you in, Mr. Pritchard, to tell you that your thesis is not acceptable."

Lawson seemed to savor the moment with such an attitude of superiority that Harry couldn't keep the aggression out of his tone. "What's wrong with it?"

"What's wrong with it is you." He pointed at Harry with the pipe. "You have done nothing but challenge me in the classroom, and your thesis insults not only me, but the law."

"Maybe that's because I was in law enforcement for fourteen years. I know how the law works—or doesn't."

"My dear Mr. Pritchard, it is not for you or me to second guess the law. The concept of a thesis is to present an idea and support it with research. I see no research notes here, no—"

"I used some of my own cases and those of fellow officers."

Lawson leaned forward smirking. "The law does not begin in the streets or in the squad room. It begins in the hallowed halls of justice." With a snap of his wrist he tossed the thesis across the desk and into Harry's lap. Then he leaned back in his chair—smugly Harry thought. "How long have you been in law school?"

"I've been taking courses off and on for the past ten years—time permitting."

"A hobby with you, obviously."

"Now, hold on—"

"If you want to graduate from this law school, Mr. Pritchard, you will conduct yourself accordingly. And you will also turn in a thesis that supports your theme which is, as I recall, Women in the Criminal Justice System: Perpetrators or Victims. And leave out the case about the woman who shot you. Too bad her aim was off." He sucked on his pipe.

Harry clenched his jaw and stretched out his legs. His left knee creaked. Be damned if he'd let a malicious old man jerk him around! Still, he was over a barrel and he knew it. Lawson was supposed to teach, counsel and guide his students. Harry decided to put the man to work.

"Okay. Which of the cases that I did present would most appeal to your sense of law?"

"Ah. Perhaps a thorough treatment of the Rossini thing. And do be imaginative. You should get an interview with the judge, the institution she's housed in, her doctors. Back up your research with tape recordings, of course. With your connections that you're so fond of quoting, perhaps you could even provide an exhibit or two, say photos of the crime scene. Law does not have to be dull."

Harry protested. "There are such things as doctor/patient ethics. Privacy—"

"Yes, there are. But an enterprising student finds a way. After all, you want to become a lawyer, don't you?"

And you, Harry thought, want me to do the work so you can produce another article to feed your ego.

"Mr. Pritchard, are you listening?" Lawson had the pipe in the corner of his mouth. He held it there. "I believe you need this degree to accept a position you've been offered with the Los Angeles County district attorney's office as investigator?"

Harry felt his temper rising. "True."

"I understand you expect to have enough credits to finally graduate at the end of the summer semester?" Lawson sucked air through his pipe.

Harry winced. "Right."

"This thesis will put you there?"

"Right again."

Lawson beamed. "Well then, Mr. Pritchard, I think we understand one another."

In his car in the student parking lot, Harry pounded on the steering column. If there was anything he hated, it was being used. Unfortunately he didn't see any way around giving Lawson what he wanted. He'd have to find one.

Harry sighed. At least the research gave him an excuse to haunt the police department. He'd see his old friends, maybe have a beer or get an invite to a poker game.

He perked up. Maybe one of the guys would even invite him home for dinner. He was tired of his own cooking. And if they told him to bring a date he could ask Felicia to come along.

He'd only had a glimpse of her over the past week— in the foyer, on the fire escape when she watered her plants; once he'd watched her striding down Catalina Street to where her car was parked.

Trouble was, he'd been out of the singles market so long, he didn't know the right way to approach a woman anymore. He didn't want to get slapped or ignored. He knew he'd have to do something to engage her attention. He needed a woman's input on the problem.

He went to see the woman whose judgement he trusted the most, his mother.

Opinionated and strong-minded, when she had come out of the fog brought on by his father's death, his mother had taken the Army insurance and bought a two-story abandoned machine shop squeezed between the borders of Little Tokyo and economically distraught downtown Los Angeles.

Though real estate salesmen had tried to talk her into buying a boxy little tract house up in Laurel Canyon, Harry Pritchard, Jr.'s widow insisted on more square footage for her money.

She had filled the first level with used furniture and created an apartment on the second floor.

Once the poverty-stricken, L.A. artist colony discovered the cheap rents in the abandoned shops and warehouses, the areas near the widow Pritchard's store became fashionable. The artists bought their furniture from his mother, ofttimes trading their own early works for her sagging sofas and mattresses.

Downtown Los Angeles went through redevelopment, land prices soared. The widow of Harry Pritchard, Jr., was suddenly sitting on a gold mine. Comfortably so.

She'd also gotten into other things—like metaphysics and astrology—of which Harry thoroughly disapproved.

The odor of the machine oil, forever embedded in the concrete floor, wafted up around him. It was a good, clean smell. American and honest. The building, however much a novelty it had been when he was a youth, was now home. He sat in an old lounge chair minus its footrest while his mother wagged finger and tongue at him.

"The problem with you, Harry, is that you don't know how to handle women. You expect us to be some elegant, virginal package waiting to be unwrapped by the knight on a white steed."

"Huh? Do I look like a knight on a white steed?"

His mother smiled. "No, and that's your most singular problem. When did you last shave?"

"I ran out of blades for my razor," he said defensively.

"So buy some. Maybe then, this girl—what's her name—?"

"Never mind."

"—will give you a second look."

"I was hoping you could suggest something more creative."

His mother sighed heavily. "You want her sympathy."

"I was thinking that would warm her up."

"And then you'd charm her into your bed?"

Harry stiffened. "She's not that type."

"You funny, funny man. Why don't you just ask her out?"

"She said no."

"Want me to look up your chart and tell you your most promising social hours?"

Harry rolled his eyes.

"Women of today don't like to feel they're being indulged or patronized. They're tired of subtlety and innuendo. They want honesty."

Harry sat up. "I'm honest."

"Not entirely. You hide your disappointments under a noble gesture or a stupid joke. You loathe admitting you're vulnerable."

"Women don't like that."

Thea laughed. "Oh, yes we do." A frown wrinkled her brow. "I suppose you're still aiming for a job with the district attorney's office. Will you have to carry a gun?"

"Not all the time. I'll just be investigating crimes after the fact."

"At least you'll be a lawyer," she said wistfully. "Your dad would be so proud."

"I'll have a law degree. That's not quite the same thing. I don't expect to sit for the bar, not at first anyway.

"If it's money—"

"I've got enough."

"But if you don't, you'll yank on the old umbilical cord?"

"Mom, if I ever get a woman I'm interested in and you in the same room, please don't talk like that."

"Sure, son." She raised her hands, palms up. "White light and peace."

Harry groaned. "Or like that, either."

"Anything you say sweet son of my loins. Now scoot. I'm expecting a client."

Harry pecked his mother on her cheek. "I'm gone."

"You know, if this girl is all that you say she is," his mother called, getting in a parting shot. "She won't be taken in by the trivial. You'll have to stimulate her brain as well as her nerve endings."

HARRY WAS NOT HAPPY. Clare and Mildred were reminiscing about Felicia's mother who they had apparently met several times. He was trying to think of reassuring things to say to Felicia and at the same time, trying to get to the bottom of his feelings.

He had accepted with alacrity Clare's invitation to join in the "to-do" she put together for Felicia. Now their chairs were so closely placed about the garden table he caught the scent of her—a warm tang like the smell of flowery musk.

Dusk was falling. In the last stray rays of the sun he could see the fine hairs on her neck. She had a creamy, slender, kissable neck; in the hollows veins pulsated.

He imagined his lips caressing those soft hollows, imagined the taste of her skin.

Felicia turned toward him. He felt blood rushing to his face.

"You're so quiet," she said, her gaze level with his own.

"Am I?" he stalled. "I had a bad day. I guess it's on my mind."

"What happened?"

"If I told you, I'd be the bore of the party."

"Oh, do tell us, Harry," chirruped Clare, continuing to talk without giving him a chance to reply. "We haven't had the opportunity to get to know you yet. It's always so much easier to know a person through their problems. Isn't that so, Alphonse?"

"It's how I met you, m'dear."

Clare grinned. Her false teeth gleamed. "Your curiosity about solving problems keeps you coming back."

"That I'll admit. Tell me where you hid the money and I'll take you dancing at the Crossbow."

Clare tilted her head, gazing up at him coyly through sparse lashes heavily coated with blue mascara. "That's not the trade I have in mind."

"Oh, looky," Mildred said. "Clare's giving us her sweet little innocent look. You nitwit, all it does is add to your double chins. Now you have four."

Clare's eyes flashed, her chin came up. "Just serve the pound cake, Mildred."

"What money?" asked Harry.

"Let me tell," Mildred said as she poured coffee all around. "Clare adds too many embellishments. We'd be here all night." She replaced the ceramic coffee pot on the table. "Clare once embezzled money from

Wells Fargo Bank. Alphonse was working for Pinkerton's. He proved Clare committed the crime but couldn't find the money. Clare wouldn't give up the money so she went to prison."

Clare huffed. "You don't know how to make a tale interesting at all, Mildred." She turned to Harry. "After I got caught I was going to give the money back, but Wells Fargo said they were going to make an example of me anyway. So I decided, why should I?"

Harry eyed the old woman with new interest. "What provoked you to steal it?"

"What provoked me, indeed! I was next in line for vice-president—I would've been the first woman to make that leap, but do you think they'd offer it to me? Oh, no...the bank president's son came back from the war and they gave the vice-presidency to him. And who do you think had to train the uppity creature? Me—that's who. Why, he could barely count up to a hundred. Certainly he couldn't make change. After I had trained him, I was given notice. The bank had to make room, you see, for all the soldiers returning from war. The way I see it, appropriating that money was nothing more than an economically sound investment—in myself."

"But, you went to jail," said Harry, doing a quick mental calculation that put the crime back in the 1940s. His mind whirled. Clare's crime, he thought, might be just the thing to add flavor to his thesis. Victim or perp? Both, he thought. It'd make for a nice twist and Clare certainly didn't seem to mind talking about it.

"Most assuredly I went to jail. I also got free room and board for the next ten years while my little nest egg just compounded interest on top of interest."

Mildred, passing slices of cake on wafer-thin plates, added an aside. "Alphonse still wants to know where Clare hid the money."

"Just out of curiosity," Alphonse injected. "I hated being outsmarted by a mere slip of a girl."

"Sexist," said Clare.

Mildred turned to Harry. "She means plain old sex. You see, Clare was so busy climbing to an executive position at the bank and stealing their money that she never had time to indulge in—"

"I never got laid," said Clare succinctly.

"Oh," said Harry, and buried his face in his coffee cup. He took a large swallow and choked.

Felicia pounded him on the back. "I should have warned you. They lace it with bourbon."

"I'm fine," he managed to say when he had caught his breath.

"Young people shock so easily these days," said Clare.

"I'm not shocked," said Harry. But he was. For all his years on the police force, this conversation just didn't seem right somehow. Clare looked like Norman Rockwell's version of a grandmother. He noticed Felicia didn't seem the least bit ruffled. In fact, her eyes were alight with silent laughter—at him.

"I could've told you what you were in for," she told him, "but I didn't want to spoil the entertainment."

"Oh, I'm entertained all right," he mouthed quietly. "Where did you hide the money, Clare?"

"I'm not telling."

"Surely the statute of limitations has run out."

"Of course it has." She chuckled. "But the money hasn't."

"How she hid the money is the *only* thing she won't tell," Mildred sniffed, reaching up to pat her pompadour.

"Look who's talking. You're no pristine Miss Muffit. Tell Harry about your little escapades."

"Oh, I rather think that wouldn't be in good taste."

Harry shot a glance at Felicia. She smiled and laid a hand on his arm. "It's just their way of showing off. You're a new audience."

He put his hand over hers, careful to keep it a kind and friendly gesture. A feeling of warmth spread throughout his body. "I love being an audience," he said.

"Will you two stop whispering," chastised Clare. "Young people are so ill-mannered."

Felicia withdrew her hand from Harry's arm. "Sorry."

Harry turned on his charm. "We were just agreeing about how elegant and entertaining you and Mildred are. And what good cooks," he added, popping a slice of cake into his mouth.

Pleased, Mildred puffed up. "I do all the cooking. Good food soothes the male spirit, I always say."

"Go on," Clare goaded. "Stop being so...coy and tell Harry just how many male spirits you've soothed."

"Clare, I wish you wouldn't rush me."

"Never mind, then. I'll tell him. Mildred and I were cell mates at Tehachapi."

Male spirits? Harry raised an eyebrow as he jumped to the obvious conclusion. "You were a hooker?"

Mildred's narrow body stiffened, her back going board straight, her bony neck elongating. "I should say not! What a horrid thing to say. I never allowed a man to get familiar with me until after we were married."

"So where's the crime in that?"

"According to the judge, the crime was that I had twenty-seven husbands sans divorce. But, really, it was during the war, there just wasn't time...and I couldn't bear to send all those sweet darlings Dear John letters. They were so comforted knowing I was here, writing to them, praying for them while they were off fighting."

Clare butted in. "Mildred's problems began when fourteen soldiers and sailors came back after the war to collect her. What really made them mad was that she'd collected all of their allotment checks, too."

"I needed the money," Mildred said in her own defense. "Everyone of those dear boys had a mother. There were gifts to buy, Mother's Day cards to send, and of course I sent care packages to each and every one of my husbands. That costs, you know. Working as a volunteer in the USO certainly didn't pay."

Harry didn't know whether to laugh or play it straight. "I'm surprised you couldn't convince the judge of your good intentions."

"Oh, I had wonderful character references from my mothers-in-law saying how they wished their sons had stayed married to me. I was the best daughter-in-law they had. Much better than the women their sons ended up with."

"Enough about us," Clare said abruptly. "Harry was going to tell us all about himself. It's so nice to have such an attractive and enterprising young man in our midst, don't you think?"

"It's nice to have someone about who can fix things," Felicia agreed.

"I'm glad there's another man under the old roof," said Alphonse. "Gets pretty hard on an old fool like myself—having to accommodate so many charming women."

Clare's claws came out. "Accommodate, how?"

Mildred cackled. "You know very well you wouldn't understand even if Alphonse drew pictures."

Chin quivering, Clare castigated them. "You're being exceedingly vulgar. I know all about sex. I've just never been a participant."

"This cake is good," said Harry.

"Don't change the subject," Mildred told him. "You'll ruin Clare's evening and I'll have to bear the brunt of her sulks."

Clare leaned forward, her faded eyes bright as beacons in the failing light. "I'll consider *any* propositions, Harry. Alphonse is my first choice, but he's being stubborn. I will not crawl into my casket a virgin and that's that!"

Harry felt a little queasy at the thought. "I...I think I'll pass. Thanks for thinking of me though." Felicia had a napkin pressed to her lips. Harry was certain she was struggling not to laugh behind it. He picked up his coffee cup and looked at her. She looked appealingly relaxed and easygoing. It had something to do with the way her hair fell loosely around her face and the way her features softened in the dusky light. He felt as if he were suddenly pulling the lid off the box where he'd stored all of his emotions. He couldn't risk it. He stood up, made polite excuses and said good-night all around.

For a brief moment Felicia seemed surprised and disappointed. He took that gratifying and unsettling thought upstairs with him.

LILA COULDN'T SEEM to dismiss the sliver of fear that lodged under her chest bone. All week long she'd tried not to think about what Sadie had done. But it kept coming back to her like a very bad penny.

When she'd attempted to discuss it, Sadie had stalked off in a snit. Now, Sadie was back, putting in an appearance as if she were some prima donna with only minutes to spare an old friend best forgotten. Agitated, Lila rinsed the soap off the dishes and stacked them to dry. She was trembling, but Sadie might as well know she had a few tricks up her own sleeve.

"If you think your going away meant I'd shut up about this, Sadie, you're wrong."

"Spare me the histrionics. I'm tired."

"The police came once because you messed up apartment six," Lila accused. "You would've left it that way again if I hadn't gone along the last time."

"I told you. I did not dump the contents of that suitcase on the floor. You're the stupid one. You should never have tidied up the place. Now, we'll have to be more careful than ever."

"Suppose Ernest caught us up there?"

"He didn't. He thought you were just coming in from the garden. Worry ought to be your middle name, Lila. You thrive on it."

Lila wrung out the dishrag and hung it over the painted rack, arranging it until the corners were perfectly aligned. "You keep secrets, Sadie. I don't like that."

"What secrets?"

"That's just it. I don't know. Why won't you tell me when you go places without me?"

Sadie snorted. "One of us has to do the shopping. You can't go two blocks without getting lost. If I didn't run the errands, you'd starve."

Lila stiffened. "From now on," she said, gathering her courage, "where you go, I go. Promise me."

Sadie was silent.

Lila pressed on. "I want your word that you won't go up to apartment six...ever...without me."

More silence.

A touch of Lila's girlhood fear returned. Frightened, yet determined, she went into the bathroom and searched the medicine cabinet. "I'll fix you, Sadie. I'll fix you good. I'm going to take the medicine the doctors gave me, then you'll have to stay away forever!"

"Wait!"

Lila's hand stilled. After a moment she heard a tremulous sigh.

"Okay. You win. You have my word."

Lila smiled. She picked up a comb and began to arrange her hair. "Clare and Mildred have invited me for coffee in the garden. Mildred baked a pound cake."

"Those two old biddies! I don't know what you see in them."

"They like me."

"I like you, too. Stay home. I don't want to have to sit through hours of their insipid chatter. It gives me a headache."

"You're spoiled, Sadie. You want everything your way. Besides, Mildred said that afterward I could listen to some of her records. Remember when Percy was in the Army? We used to go dancing."

"I remember he used to dance with every woman but you."

"He danced with me," Lila insisted. She leaned toward the mirror to apply lipstick.

"For heaven's sake, Lila. You're smearing that stuff all over your face. Here, let me do it."

Lila retreated. But once the lipstick was in place, her vacant eyes gleamed, renewed with images and memories so fresh, the events seemed to have occurred only moments ago. "I married Percy, didn't I?"

"Yes, and you put us through hell. Don't go off anywhere now, Lila. I'm not going to entertain Clare and Mildred for you. I refuse."

Lila viewed herself in the mirror, primping like a teenager. "Don't worry. I'm sure they wouldn't like you, either."

She pranced out of the apartment with a sly smile on her lips, but by the time she got to the back stoop, the garden was empty. She stood there in the dim light trying to remember what it was she'd meant to do.

"I'VE BEEN DELEGATED to find out if you were offended by Clare and Mildred," Felicia said when Harry opened his door to her.

"Offended? Me?"

"You did rush off."

He looked pained. Be honest, his mother had said. "To tell you the truth, it did shave a bit off my ego to have an eighty-year-old make a pass at me."

"Take it as a compliment."

"Compliment, hell! Had I been up to it, you would've seen the first two-minute mile run by a cripple."

Felicia laughed. "You're not crippled."

"You don't think so?"

"You seem very capable to me."

"You want to come in? I was just rattling around in the kitchen." He went behind the counter and cleared a space. "I can offer you beer or a soft drink."

Felicia hesitated. "I'd like to ask your opinion on something."

"I'm your man." He held up the cans. "Which?"

"Cola is fine," she said and crossed to his kitchen counter. It was a duplicate of her own, but there the similarities between their apartments dwindled. Harry's was cluttered with the debris of his life; books, typewriter, exercise machines, discarded food cartons. Typical bachelor, Felicia thought.

"Did gremlins visit you again?" he asked.

"No. I've had to do my own dishes and dust under my own bed."

He grinned. "So what's worrying you?" He waited.

"I can't seem to locate a death certificate."

"Your mother's?"

"No, my brother's."

"Write to Vital Statistics. They'll locate it."

"I tried Vital Statistics. There's a record of his birth but not of his death."

"In that case, he's alive."

"That couldn't be."

"Why not?"

"You see, my mom never even mentioned that I had a brother. If he were alive, what would that say about my parents? That they gave him up for...for adoption?''

"You want me to check on him for you?''

"I thought—would you mind? Police officers, even former police officers, have connections, don't they?''

"I have some friends. I'll ask around.''

"I have his birth certificate. Would that help?''

It wouldn't, Harry knew. "It's not necessary. What's his name?''

"Thomas Adam Bennington.''

"Age?''

"Twenty-nine. He'll be thirty on June seventh.''

"I'll see what I can find out. Try not to get your hopes up, though. If someone doesn't want to be found...'' He left the thought hanging and started thinking desperately how to lighten the mood.

"I understand.''

"Could I ask you a question now?'' There was a determined glint in his eyes.

"Sure,'' she answered cautiously.

"Do you believe in love at first sight?''

"I—''

"What's your position on couples making love after a fight? Say—in the shower? Or do you think sex should always be in the bedroom?''

"You *were* the one who messed up my apartment!''

He opened a loaf of bread then met her gaze with a twinkle in his eye. "Would you like a potted meat sandwich?''

"Excuse me. I have to go,'' Felicia said, flustered by the turn their conversation had taken. She turned to leave.

"Can you manage a two-minute mile?" His teasing words ricocheted softly off her back.

Felicia halted, and turned, suddenly suspicious of Harry's motives. "That wasn't nice."

"Neither are those two old ladies. If they were my grandmothers— And you laughed at me."

"You mean it's all right for old men to talk about sex, but not old ladies?"

"Exactly."

Her face was still a light shade of pink. "No wonder you're divorced."

Harry winced. "That's a low blow."

"A man thinks just because he's good-looking he can get away with anything."

His heartbeat soared. "You think I'm good looking?"

"In a rough kind of way."

"In that case, how about that picnic? Tomorrow."

"I'm working with Zelda. Sorry."

"You don't sound sorry."

"Well, maybe I'm just not your kind of woman."

"How do you know?"

"You told me. Remember—under thirty, over thirty? That only leaves—dead. Or—" she regarded him with mischief "—maybe, Clare."

Harry followed her to the door and watched her cross the hall. "I take back everything I said. I'm crazy about you. I want to take you home to meet my mother."

"If you're that hard up, you ought to hang around in singles bars."

Harry blanched. "Those dens of sin and who-knows-what-all? Forget it. Anyway, I'm not hard up."

"Wonderful. Then I guess I won't have to worry about you being lonely." She closed her door. Harry listened for the snap of the safety latch. It came.

He rapped lightly on her door. "Was it something I said?"

"It was everything you said." Her answer came muffled, but distinct.

He heard a shuffling noise behind him...faint, and to his ears, furtive. He walked to the stairwell and leaned over the bannister. "Who's down there?"

Footsteps clattered, a door slammed.

Harry paused on the top step. One of the old biddies eavesdropping, he surmised. Was he going to let them, or Felicia have the last word? Hell, no! He banged on Felicia's door, police-style.

She opened it at the length of the chain. "Darn it! You scared the daylights out of me."

"I want a word with you."

"I've had all the words I want with you."

"I put the hinges on your door, I can take 'em off."

She unlatched the chain, threw the door open and glared up at him. "You've been spoiling for a fight since the day you moved in. So fight. If you think I can be bullied—"

"You're a regular little spitfire."

"Don't call me little. I'm big in spirit."

"Is that a true statement?"

"Try me and see," she warned. She watched his golden eyes darken to amber, filling with anguish, perhaps? Felicia wasn't certain.

"Okay," he said. "I like you. I don't exactly know how to go about asking you out, because I don't know what appeals to women—you, in particular. I've sort of been keeping an eye out when you come and go, trying to think up things. You're so—so self-contained and . . . unflappable.

"I'm thirty-eight years old. You make me feel like an adolescent. Tongue-tied and weak-kneed. That's about where I'm at." He cleared his throat. "How's your spirit holding up?"

Felicia leaned against the doorjamb. He'd just confessed to vulnerabilities she hadn't thought he had. It diffused her anger, disarmed her. "Just fine."

"What about that picnic?"

"I told you—"

"Seven-thirty? I'll pack candles."

"A picnic in the dark?"

"I have an errand to attend to first. I'd like it if you'd ride along. We may not need the candles. I'll even promise not to talk about sex."

She felt an extraordinary compulsion to say yes, and yet a tension held her limbs in its grip. Harry thrust out his hand. Felicia's stayed limp by her side. He grabbed it and pumped. "It's a date."

"Harry . . ."

Her eyes met his and held his gaze. "This is how you're supposed to do it." She went up on her toes and briefly pressed her lips to his.

Chapter Six

Felicia gazed at the Navaho rug pattern that gleamed wet and colorful in the late-afternoon sun. The old wooden porch had taken on new life.

"I'm glad that job's done!" Zelda said as she loaded paint cans into the trunk of her car. "My knees feel like I've got mattress burn!"

Realization that the job was done brought thoughts of Harry full force into Felicia's mind. "I have a date tonight," she said.

Zelda gaped. "What! You kept that a secret all day? How could you?"

"Did you give me a chance to say anything?"

"I can't believe it. A date. Who is the lucky guy? One of the engineers at work? I haven't seen you making eyes at anybody."

"I'm too busy to make eyes at anyone. Anyway, it's only Harry."

"Only Harry? He needs nurturing? What with his injuries and all?"

"Cut the sarcasm."

"He's going to eat you alive."

"No, he's really quite nice. He's just not very good with women."

"He said that? And you believed him?"

"I thought you liked him."

"I do. But you're vulnerable right now—what with your mother dying, trying to find where your brother's buried—"

"Harry's going to look into that for me. Besides, I'm no more vulnerable than you." Or Harry, she thought. "It's just a picnic."

"It'll be dark before you can get near a park."

"Harry's bringing candles."

Zelda stared at her friend. "You know what? I'd better get Thea to put a rush on your horoscope. You may be in big trouble."

"What kind of trouble could Harry be?"

"Heart trouble," Zelda said emphatically. "I'll be over first thing in the morning to hear all about it."

"No, you won't. I have work to catch up on."

"You're going to have this grand love affair and not tell me one word?"

Felicia took one last glance at their art work. "We're going on a picnic. I'll tell you what the ants did. Promise." She held out her hand. "Divvy up the money. I have to stop by Von's on the way home. If I want something other than potted meat tonight, I'll have to provide it."

"I suppose all Harry has to bring are the candles— and his body."

In the spirit of friendship, Felicia held her tongue.

FELICIA DISCOVERED she was second guessing every thought she had about Harry. Yet she felt a pull toward him unlike what she'd felt for any other man. There was the surface Harry, sometimes rough, sometimes gentle and caring, as if he himself was not sure of which image to present. And just when her confusion about him was at its height, he'd give her a peek at his other aspects, his vulnerabilities. She didn't know which way to play it.

Yet here she was, sitting next to him, with an uncommon airy feeling in the pit of her stomach and a pulse of excitement charging up her spine.

Harry spoke, putting an end to her reverie. "I feel like I won the lottery and you're the grand prize."

She raised an eyebrow. "How often do you date, Harry?"

"I had two dates with my wife before we got married—one of those whirlwind things. I haven't exactly had the opportunity since then. What with military service, police work, taking law courses every chance I get . . . And getting shot has taken a year and a half out of my life." His sigh seemed to erupt from the very depths of his soul.

The car they were in was a yellow 1957 Ford Thunderbird, a two-seater, with a hard top. Felicia didn't know much about cars, beyond the fact that her own ten-year-old Dodge was forever needing tires, gas, oil, batteries, or fuel pumps, but she was certain the Thunderbird was a classic—and costly.

"Out of work, but not destitute, by the looks of this car," she said, pleased with her smooth delivery. She sounded interested—but not too interested.

"Mom took this car in trade for a couple of beds from a pair of hippies back in the Sixties. She gave it to me for my sixteenth birthday. It was a wreck, but I kept fixing this, fixing that . . ." He tapped the dash. "Good ol' Bessie. She's been with me through thick and thin. Mostly thin. But I'm not exactly out of work. I do a little of this 'n' that, I stay afloat."

"You're a man of many talents."

"Not as many as I'd like. Or maybe I should say I don't have the kind of talent that most women seem to like."

"Oh? What kind of talent would that be?"

"Upward mobility." He glanced at her. "So, what kind of man do you like?"

"Those who are thoughtful, caring and like me back," she said, smiling impishly. Harry felt a small stab of satisfaction. She was teasing him, not being critical. He smiled, then turned his attention to the heavy homeward-bound traffic.

He had shaved, Felicia noticed, which surprisingly did not do much to soften the roguish image he projected.

It was the artist in her that made those observations. He was undeniably attractive, a man of strength, perhaps even dangerous. Contrary to those observations was the notion she couldn't shake that Harry was a man unable to look after himself properly. It was the woman in her that noticed that; warmed to it, in fact. Of course, it could be an act.

He was most assuredly efficient behind the wheel of his car.

They were on Colorado Street. He slowed. "Look there," he pointed. "Remember the Hillside stranglings? That old upholstery shop is where Bianchi and Bono did some of the women in."

Felicia felt a jolt in her heart. "Did you work on cases like that?"

"Yeah." His expression changed, going hard as he tossed his mind's eye on pictures of victims he'd seen. "I never did get used to the destruction."

"That's an odd way of putting it."

"Not odd...exact. That's what crime does...
destroys companies, property, people, flesh, families—" He swung his gaze back to Felicia—a brief
look, but it spoke of depths within him few knew existed. "But all right, let's forget crime. Tell me all
about yourself. Start when you were born." He paused
and looked at her reflectively. "Is that a corny line? I
read it in one of those books that tell you how to get a
conversation going."

"You don't need the book. You do quite nicely on
your own."

"So talk," he said. "Have you ever been married?"

"No."

"In love?"

She hesitated. "Maybe once or twice."

"Maybe? Don't you know?"

"We drifted apart. I've never—there was always
something missing."

There was a bone-deep longing in her voice. It made
Harry take his eyes from the road for a moment to
catch the look on her face. Her expression matched
her tone: quiet and lost. She had a defenselessness
about her, a fragility that touched him, that made him
want to reassure her. He looked away, afraid that she
might sense what he was thinking. The irony was that
he didn't know whether she was cold-blooded or pas-
sionate: whether he could comfort her or not. He felt
a lump in his throat every time he looked at her, and
he cursed himself for a romantic fool. "I've picked a
fantastic spot for our picnic. Up in the hills."

He meant Beverly Hills. Felicia had never been in
that exclusive domain of the rich and famous, so she
held her tongue as Harry turned onto Benedict Can-

yon. He knew the main roads and the back roads and points of interest. At the top of Bella Drive, he stopped and pointed across the narrow canyon to some well-lighted grounds. "See that house. That's where Charles Manson's followers killed Sharon Tate, Abigail Folger, the coffee heiress, and three others."

Felicia shivered. It was almost full dark and this talk of violent crime frightened her. What did she know—really know—about Harry Pritchard? "I don't like hearing about things like that. It's gory. You're scaring me."

"Damn. Sorry." He really did sound chagrined. "It's just that crime scenes are what I know." He put the car in gear. "One terrific picnic spot coming up."

"It's not isolated is it?"

He hesitated. "Not exactly."

"I'm not hungry, Harry. Let's go back. We can picnic in the garden."

"You're not scared of me?"

"I don't think touring murder scenes makes for a fun time."

"You're safe with me. Think of me as your knight in shining armor."

"That's just it. I don't want to be put in any position in which I have to be rescued."

"You think I'm that kind of guy?"

"I'm beginning to wonder. Where are we going anyway?"

"I told you I had an errand to run before the picnic."

"So, tell me about the errand," she said, her voice full of suspicion.

"Almost there," he said, turning onto what looked to Felicia to be a private road. He followed an unkempt lane so overgrown that shrubs and tall grasses brushed the sides of the car. The lane opened out into a landscape as equally unkempt but alight with moon glow and stars. The moon's path revealed a house, huge and looming where it was caught in shadow.

"We're going to picnic here? This looks like somebody's estate."

"It is." He parked in the lee of some great old rhododendrons that had long since lost their blooms.

A shiver worked its way up Felicia's spine. "It's too dark here. And what about your errand?"

"Just sit tight for a minute." His voice was low, his eyes on the house. He went to the trunk of the car, pulled out the picnic supplies, laid a blanket on the ground, stuck the candles in the soft earth and lighted them. That done, he ushered Felicia out of the car. "Isn't that nice?"

Outside the glow of the flickering candles, Felicia saw little. "No."

She sat cross-legged on the blanket, her eyes shifting constantly against the possibility of creepy-crawlies—or worse.

"What did you bring?" Harry asked. He inspected the sandwiches she'd made. "Roast beef? I love roast beef."

"Who lives in the house, Harry? I can see a light in that upstairs window."

"I thought you'd never ask. You want to meet her?" He went to the car and tooted the horn; several ear-shattering blasts. Then he returned to Felicia's side. "She'll be out in a minute."

The sloping overgrown lawn went suddenly bright with security lights. "Your mother lives here, doesn't she?" Felicia said, understanding dawning. "You didn't have to go to such convoluted methods to get me here. You could've just asked."

Harry was having second thoughts about involving Felicia in his errand. He'd originally seen it as an adventure, something different. But suddenly he wasn't so sure it had been a good idea.

The carved front doors under the portico of the house opened. An old woman appeared on the threshold. She had a broom in her hand. "Who's out there?"

"It's just me and Felicia," Harry called.

The old woman took a few faltering steps toward them. "Who?"

"Harry, you've probably scared the poor dear to death." Felicia stood and walked toward the woman.

"Felicia...come back here," Harry ordered. He caught up to her and grabbed her arm. "Just wait right here, please."

The old woman wore two dresses, the hem of one hanging far below the other. She clutched the broom handle tightly as she approached them. "Who the hell are you? Get off my property."

Harry stepped forward, glancing from the woman to a paper he held in his hand. "You aren't Mrs. ...?" He mumbled a name that sounded awfully like his own.

"I'm Elvira McMahon, and this is my land. Get off it."

Harry looked perplexed. "But—" he held out the paper. "—look, it says right here—"

The old woman snatched the paper from his hand. "I don't give a fig what it says—git!"

"Sure thing, Mrs. McMahon." Taking Felicia by the elbow, Harry retreated with alacrity. He began rolling up the blanket. "You have been served with a subpoena. See you in court."

"Court? What are you talking—" The woman looked down at the paper. A string of epithets erupted from her.

"Into the car," Harry said to Felicia, taking her arm to hurry her along. Mrs. McMahon began swinging the broom, catching Harry a wallop across his back. "Hey!" he cried. "That's assault!"

"Assault? Assault? You low-life—"

She chased them until they were in the car and the doors locked. Harry backed the car all the way down the narrow lane. At the main road he stopped. "You weren't in love with those roast beef sandwiches were you? How does a steak sound? You earned it."

Felicia sat rigid at his side, fury as much her companion as fear, which was only beginning to subside. "What was that all about? What did you do to that woman! We could've been *killed*!"

"With a broom? Sweetheart, that's mild."

"What was that paper?"

"A civil subpoena. I deliver them for law firms. You can't have your day in court you know, unless your opponent has been notified to be there. That old biddie didn't pay her staff for almost a year, then she fired them. Now they're suing her for back wages. She's rich as Croesus and just as stingy. She's been dodging that subpoena for ten weeks."

"You mean our picnic was just an elaborate charade to help you deliver a subpoena?"

Harry had a sinking feeling in his gut. "I thought we'd do a little something different."

"It was different all right. Take me home! And, don't you ever speak to me again!"

"Justice was done. Aren't you on the side of justice?"

"You betrayed our friendship! Don't you see that?"

Harry slumped over the steering wheel. "Betrayed? Wouldn't you have gone along if I'd asked?"

"No! You're the most thick-headed, insensitive brute I've ever met. You're everything that old lady called you! And to think I was beginning to like you."

"You were?"

"Take me home this instant!"

"Be reasonable. There must be some way I can get back on your good side."

"There is. Drop dead."

He ground the gears and spun onto the highway. "I hate a woman who can't see the humor in a situation."

"I hate a man who takes advantage of me. You asked me out on false pretenses."

"But I'm ready and willing to take you out. That's not false pretenses."

"Stop the car and let me out."

"Stop the car and let you out? Get real. There's a world full of rapists, kidnappers and serial killers that prey on hitchhikers out there. And, I'm much nicer company than they are. Let me show you. I'm responsible for you."

"You call being sneaky and underhanded nice?"

"Gee whiz. You object to a guy making a living?"

"I don't like trickery."

"Let me tell you something—trickery is what the law is all about. Even the worst attorney can twist his version of events around the facts and make it seem like truth."

"And that appeals to you?"

"Stop trying to make everything I do sound dirty. What appeals to me is keeping people from doing that. Keeping them from evading the law. I delivered that subpoena fair and square. The good guys don't win often enough. They need help. Especially the little guys, the ones on the edge, who're just trying to make a living to feed their kids or pay the light bill."

"You think you're one of the little good guys?"

"Hell, no! I'm talking about yard men and dishwashers and housekeepers and waitresses that get stiffed. Regular folks. Good folks."

"You're wonderfully altruistic."

Harry heard her sarcasm and shut up. He couldn't think how to convince her of his sincerity.

Felicia maintained a stiff silence all the way back to Pasadena. She let herself out of the car the moment he came to a full stop.

Harry expelled an ironic sigh, and made one last try to get a second chance. "Aren't you forgetting something? You kissed me."

Felicia rolled her eyes heavenward. "A peck on the lips. It didn't mean a thing."

He reached for her arm as she turned to leave, but jerked his hand back before touching her as if he'd been torched. Holding on to her wouldn't make her stay, it would just make her angry. His only weapons were his words. "It meant something to me. In my book a woman just doesn't go around kissing a guy unless it means something."

Felicia was obviously resisting the urge to gape. "You march to a Neanderthal drummer, Harry. It's no wonder your wife divorced you."

"It's a good thing I'm studying to become a lawyer or I'd never see that for the double-talk it is."

"I mean it."

"Sounds like an escape clause to me."

"You have escape clauses on the brain. I've never had anyone suspect my sincerity, or my art, for that matter."

They finished breakfast in companionable silence. Felicia stacked the dishes in the sink. "I have to go over to the float barns this morning."

"Suppose I don't want to let you out of my sight?" Moist, warm places inside Felicia began to tingle. "You'll have to."

He knew he should let the matter drop. He should have learned from her signals when not to proceed further. But he couldn't seem to help himself. "Escape clauses?"

"Are you trying to pick a fight?"

"No. But what about last night?"

She wanted to tell him that last night had been momentous in her life. A milestone. That what she felt for him she had never felt for any other man. But then he'd accuse her of looking for commitment, like the over-thirty women he'd talked about. He had her boxed in.

"I was crazy about you last night," he said. "I'm still crazy about you this morning."

"But I have work to do."

"From the ashes of passion arises the career woman," he said, bitterness riding every syllable. "I suppose you didn't notice how neatly you fit in my arms?" She'd fit neatly into his heart, too, and it was scaring the hell out of him.

Felicia was taken aback. "I did notice."

"Are you trying to punish yourself or me?" he asked, knowing some quirk within himself was forcing an upset in the delicate balance of their emerging relationship. He struggled to find a way to regain lost ground. "I've learned compromise since my divorce. If you need to get ready for work, hop in the shower, I'll scrub your back."

"I need time to absorb what happened between us."

"And then what? Do we explore our relationship?" And because he was thinking of it himself and it scared him, he accused her, "Next, you'll be mentioning marriage."

Her chin went up an inch. "With you? On the basis of a one-night stand? I wouldn't dare."

"That's what you think we shared? A one-night stand?" Hurt, he heaved himself off the stool and went to get his shirt and shoes. When he returned to the living room Felicia was standing by the door, holding it open for him.

He walked out without speaking.

Felicia slammed the door on his heels.

"I JUST NEED someone to talk to," Felicia said into the telephone.

"You picked the wrong morning for it," Zelda said tensely. "I'm supposed to have an exciting romantic interlude today."

"You have somebody there?"

"Not yet, but he will be. I'm expecting a call any minute now."

Felicia sank back into the sofa cushions. Calling Zelda had been a mistake. "You mean your horoscope said you'd have a romantic interlude. Zelda, you're planning your whole life according to a piece of paper!''

"It's my life. You're like the weather, Felicia, you just happen. What's the difference between me looking at my horoscope before making decisions and you waiting to find your center?''

Felicia closed her eyes. "Maybe nothing. I'll see you at work tomorrow.''

"Wait up. You sound upset. I can spare a minute. What's on your mind?''

Felicia hesitated. "Harry Pritchard.''

"The picnic was a wipeout?''

"Mostly.'' She didn't want to get into the specifics. "We're not speaking.''

"Do you want to?''

"I guess. I don't know.''

"Poor Felicia,'' crooned Zelda. "When will you ever learn? You have a tendency to overestimate a man's attention span.''

"I don't think that's it at all.'' Of course it was. Harry wanted a short-term affair, she wanted something longer—as in life. And if she allowed herself to consider him a permanent fixture, she'd only end up getting hurt.

"Astrology would help. Find out his birth sign. He may be a Capricorn or a Taurus. In which case, your being a Gemini—''

"Zelda, I have to go. I have some things to do around here, then I'm off to the barns. I've got to check some work on the floats against schematics.''

"All right. I'll try to hurry Thea along on your chart, Felicia. At least then you'll know your best times for romantic opportunity.''

"I'm not looking for romantic opportunity.''

"Whether you want to believe it or not, Felicia, you are. You want to be kissed, cuddled and adored. Every woman does. The proof is right there under your roof. Clare is so old she could pass for a mummy and she's still looking. So, lie to me if it makes you feel better, but stop lying to yourself."

"Sometimes I wonder why we continue to be best friends," Felicia said, wincing at how sharp her voice sounded.

Zelda's laughter came clearly through the wires. "That's easy. We tolerate each other's peculiarities. Now, you just have to learn to tolerate Harry's."

"But he brings out the worst in me!"

"In whose eyes? His or yours?"

"Enough philosophy!"

"Okay," said Zelda. "Bye."

"I DIDN'T WAKE YOU, did I?" Harry asked his mother.

"You don't sound bright and cheery, Harry. What's the problem?"

"Nothing."

"I see. Then, to what do I owe this call?"

"Why can't more women be like you?"

Thea laughed. "You mean why don't women put up with you being pompous, morose and spoiled? Your date with your new friend didn't go well?"

Harry slumped in his chair. "The beginning went okay. I took her with me to deliver a subpoena."

"Haven't you heard of ordinary dates like movies, dancing, candlelight dinners?"

"I took candles."

Thea laughed. "Harry, dear, all you need do is find some common ground with this girl. Once you find it, stand on it. And don't push her off it, either. You're looking for someone to share your life with. Admit it."

"I did that once. Look where it got me—divorced."

"You can't hold that against every woman you meet." Thea sighed. "I wish you had brothers and sisters, Harry. I really do."

Harry jumped at the change of topic. "What do you know about twins, or more specifically, twins separated at birth?"

"Twins. Let me think. Twinship lends itself to uncanny affinities, or so the psychologists say. Lonely children fantasize a lost twin somewhere, the perfect companion, a soul mate, or another self. They've had documented ESP experiences."

"Trust you to know that."

"You did ask, dear."

"If somebody just found out she had a twin brother, would it be important to her to find him?"

"I would say so, yes. Are you taking up private investigating, too?"

"I'm just doing somebody a favor."

Thea paused. "I see. We're not talking about two different girls here, are we?"

Harry vacillated. "She's not into astrology or ESP. She's very down to earth. Practical."

"Harry, my love, she can't be overly practical, not if she's even on the periphery of your life. And I'm practical too. I do own a perfectly respectable furniture shop. I'm thinking about selling it, by the way."

Harry felt shocked. "Sell? But the shop is home. You live there."

"I can live anywhere. Right now I'm thinking about Florida. There's this little psychic village called Cassadaga. I'd like to check it out—"

"I just can't see you pulling up stakes—"

"I can. Have you been listening to the smog alerts lately? And I have friends who still haven't recovered from the San Francisco quake. That's scary. You're a slave to your genes, Harry. Grow into them. When you want to know the best time to woo your new friend just give me a call."

"I'll manage that on my own, thanks."

"Wonderful. Harry, don't spend the day sulking."

"It's a good thing you're my mother," Harry said.

"Yes, isn't it?" Thea replied, laughing. "At least you're certain of the role of one woman in your life." She rang off.

His mother was planning to move all the way cross-country? He felt a wrench in his gut, as if she were already gone. It gave him extra insight into what Felicia was feeling at the more permanent loss of her own mother. Common ground, he thought.

HE AND FELICIA exited their respective apartments at the same moment. But for all the attention Felicia paid him, he might as well have been a two-legged gnat.

That didn't mean she wasn't aware of him. Because he was hard on her heels, Felicia rushed down the stairs and along the narrow hall to the front entrance where she ran headlong into Ernest Ross.

"Why, Felicia," he crooned. "How nice to see you again."

She would have escaped despite her stumble, but Ernest reached out to steady her with a hand so there was no avoiding him. Felicia couldn't help it. She didn't like the man. He was too slick, too smooth. He had a big florid face with a responsible little mustache and small beady eyes gone flat. She had always felt uneasy in his presence. She knew it was uncharitable to judge the man on his looks and that it was even more unfair because he had always been unfailingly polite to her when they chanced to meet.

"Nice to see you again," she said. Harry came out and stood at Felicia's side. His face betrayed no emotion, but she sensed something in the way he stood there, near her. He gave the impression that he and she were a duo.

Ernest gave Felicia a broad grin, as if they were accomplices in some way, and she had no way of undoing the illusion. "Introduce me to your friend, Felicia."

She waved a hand in Harry's direction without benefit of a glance. "Harry Pritchard, a new tenant. Ernest Ross, Lila's son."

While Ernest held Harry captive, shaking his hand, Felicia hurried halfway down the block to her car.

The engine refused to turn over. It also refused to spume, sputter, or growl. Such balkiness was not unexpected. She no longer indulged the old car's eccentricities with costly repairs. Resigned, she got out and lifted the hood.

"Trouble?" Harry asked, behaving as if he were just a passerby and not following her.

"Go away."

He glanced at the engine. "Looks like the battery cables need cleaning."

She knew it was implausible to stand there in the street with her car's hood up and expect him to disappear. She went to the trunk, opened it, scrounging for screwdriver and rag.

Harry admired the view she presented; jeans drawn taut over slender hips, breasts emphasizing their fullness as she leaned forward. "Let me do that for you."

"No thanks. I'm perfectly capable of managing it myself."

"I've no doubt about that."

"Good."

"Give a little, Felicia."

"Why should I?"

"Well, we're neighbors for one thing."

She stared up at him. "That's my line."

"So is one-night stand. Suppose I told you it makes me unhappy to see you unhappy."

Her mind refused to accept it—refused even to consider it. "Do I look unhappy?"

"Actually, yes. Now, let me do my good deed for the day."

Felicia pretended indifference. "If you insist."

She watched as he loosened the battery cables, then took a pocketknife from his jeans and began to scrape away the crusted collection of acids and dirt from the cable connections.

Truthfully, and she suspected she was going to have to face more than one truth in the matter of Harry Pritchard, it felt good to have him solving the car problem for her.

Even as this thought struck her, the truth was beginning to solidify, blocking out everything except a sense of panic. For her, there had been no man in her life before him. There were things about him she found endearing: the way he tilted his head when he was concentrating; the way his eyes gleamed as if he held secrets dear; his smile, especially when it was directed at her alone.

Perhaps going to bed with him had not been as foolish as she'd first thought. Consciously she decided not to look too far ahead to the pitfalls, regardless of how obvious and deep.

"Try it," he said.

"What?" she asked, startled.

"Turn on the ignition. See if it catches."

She did. The motor caught and purred to life. And then, because she'd made her decision, she heard herself asking, "Want to ride along to the float barns with me? My work won't take long and afterward I can show you around. Good deeds deserve a reward."

He hesitated, suspicious of her turn in mood. Scraping battery cables didn't seem a strong enough reason for her to butter him up, or to make him forget his bruised feelings. "I was on my way to buy the Sunday papers."

"We can do that, too."

"And some doughnuts," he said, in an offhanded tone that suggested he didn't much care one way or the other.

"You're playing hard to get, Harry."

Harry recalled his mother's advice against sulking. "A man has to use whatever tried and true resources are available to him."

Felicia shook her head. "Harry, if you could package your ego, you'd be a millionaire."

He laughed. Being close to Felicia went right to his nerves and made his hands long to be doing things. He reached across and stroked her neck, feeling a secret pleasure at her barely perceptible shiver.

"I didn't like the way that guy looked at you."

"Which guy?"

"Ernest Ross."

Felicia responded with a slightly teasing remark. "We've finally found something we agree on. I don't like the way he looks at me, either. He gives me the creeps." The words were no sooner out of her mouth than she felt conscience-stricken. "But he *is* devoted to his mother."

"So are most deviants," Harry said conclusively.

On the way to the barns, conversation skipped and drifted from topic to topic. After a while Harry decided to establish their common ground. He mentioned his mother. "She's thinking about moving to Florida."

"You're close to your mother?"

"I like her. I guess that's close. We talk."

"I was close to my mother, too. When I'd visit we used to snuggle up in bed under the covers, sip hot chocolate and talk the night away."

Harry gave that some thought. Snuggling up with Felicia sounded good to him. "I know I can't take your mother's place, but I brew a mean cup of chocolate."

Felicia kept her gaze on traffic. "Why exactly did you divorce?"

"Shall I invent details to make myself look better?"

"No."

"I worked long hours, went to school in my spare time. Rita didn't like being alone. Before the insurance salesman, there was a certified public accountant."

"How did that make you feel?"

"Worse than stupid. I'd plan a weekend getaway for us and she'd go all selfless, saying she knew I had to study or work on a case. I thought she was incredibly understanding. What I didn't know was my plans conflicted with her trysts. I don't know, maybe we outgrew each other."

"You sound sad."

"A guy likes to think he can get it right the first time."

Felicia heard the self-chastisement in his voice. Her spirits plummeted. She wanted to offer him commiseration but he might think it commonplace. The alternative was to tell him that she found him different, special and unique. But she didn't have the courage to say that. Not yet anyway.

Because it was Sunday, she had her choice of parking spaces. She chose one nearest the entrance in deference to Harry's knees. Not, she thought, that he had been complaining. It was only a small gesture of caring. Somehow she felt compelled to make it up to him for Rita's certified public accountant.

Harry was impressed with the size of the buildings. He looked up. "You could put a fleet of planes in one of these."

"A fleet of floats," she corrected.

He followed as she unlocked a side door and stepped in. "Be careful," she warned. "It's dark."

Harry stopped in his tracks. The smell of machine oil and old sawed lumber assaulted his nose. The silence inside the building was so stark, it was eerie. Monolithic structures of no readily discernible shape soared upward in the deep gloom. He was reluctant to step out of the shaft of sunlight the open door afforded. The building creaked and groaned as if it were alive. He heard a scurrying sound from deep within the belly of the barn. His stomach twinged. Of course, he wasn't scared. He'd been in much more nervy situations than a dark room with odd sounds and strange shapes. "Turn on the damned lights!" he called out to Felicia.

Her laughter came to him faintly, as if she were in a tunnel. "I'm doing that now."

A moment later he was bathed in light. Wire and steel structures dwarfed him. Bolted to huge, flat float beds, they seemed to take up all the air space. He glanced up at the tallest that soared ceilingward. "Awesome," he said when Felicia rejoined him.

"I know. Television has a way of shrinking the size of floats. Some are two stories high and just as long."

"You actually design these things?" A new note of respect was in his voice.

Though slightly embarrassed, Felicia felt herself blooming under his unrestrained admiration. "From the animation to where every single flower is placed. This year the parade theme is comedy, fun and whimsy."

"I'm impressed."

"Finally."

"Hold on, I've been impressed before. After last night—"

Her bloom wilted. "Why do men always want to talk about sex?"

He gazed at her with an expression midway between mild pain and resigned tolerance. "Because we like it?"

"Disgusting." She turned, heading toward the senior engineer's office.

Harry followed. "You're saying you don't?"

"I'm not saying that." She tossed the comment over her shoulder. "But, I don't need to talk about it."

"Men are different." He noted how stiff her back was. "Say something nice, why don't you? Let me know you're not really mad. My ego is somewhere down around my ankles."

Nothing. Her tennis shoes made no sound upon the oil-and grease-stained concrete floor.

"If I could go back on the police force, you'd get your wish," he said.

"What wish is that?"

"Well, every fifty-seven hours day and night, a police officer is killed in the line of duty."

Felicia rolled her eyes heavenward. "Give it up, Harry."

"I'm just trying to get back on your good side."

"Why?"

"I don't want to walk home. My knees hurt."

"Funny, they don't seem to bother you when you've got the upper hand."

"Do I ever have the upper hand with you?"

"What are you getting at?"

He grinned. "Can I take you home to meet my mother?"

She held her breath for a moment. "Implying?"

His smile slipped. "Nothing. I just want you to meet my mom."

"Oh. Well, sometime. Wait here, I'll only be a minute." She disappeared into the office. A moment later she reappeared with a roll of schematics under her arm. Harry was nowhere to be seen.

"Harry?"

His head popped up from the operator well of a float bed. "How the hell does anyone see to drive these monsters?"

"They don't. The driver's keep their eye on the pink line painted down the middle of the parade route. Think you could manage one?"

"I can drive anything on wheels."

"I'll put your name up to the senior engineer. He's always looking for volunteers."

Harry backpedaled. "I always watch the game on New Year's."

"It might be exciting. You could drive a float full of beautiful women—"

He climbed out of the float pit and lowered himself to the floor. Then put his hands on her shoulders and pulled her toward him. "I'd rather have you."

Felicia stood very still in his arms.

He lifted his gaze from her face to the floats, the bits and pieces of machinery and wire shapes that, once dressed with flowers, were to be clowns and animals and effigies of well-known comics.

She could feel the shape and texture and heat of his hands through the shirt she wore. When he ran his palms lightly down her arms she ached for him. He smelled of soap and after-shave. To her it was an aphrodisiac. She had to keep the conversation going—somehow—or she'd succumb. "Do you still want doughnuts?"

"I want to kiss you. I have all morning."

"You're changing the subject."

"It needs changing." His lips touched hers, his tongue thrusting and probing. When his lips moved along her cheek to her ear, he whispered, "Let's forget the doughnuts and go back to your place."

A part of Felicia wanted to agree, but a niggling inner voice said no. Her stomach gathered into knots. Why, she wondered couldn't she just say yes, and take all that was being offered her? Her silence brought Harry's head up sharply, and he pulled away from her. "Well?"

She felt vulnerable in every way. "Let's stick to the game plan. Doughnuts and newspaper."

"Right," he said with an air of resignation, knowing with certainty that a doughnut was not going to satisfy his current appetite.

While Felicia unrolled her schematics, made notes and checked drawings against work completed, Harry watched her.

"Stop staring at me," she said.

"I was just trying to discern the limits of your obstinate phase—how it starts, how long it lasts."

"I'm not obstinate. I'm the easiest person in the world to get along with."

Harry knew where disputing that would get him. He gazed at the wire mesh sculptures. "How do you make the flowers stick on those things?"

"We spray the entire float with polyethylene, the same sort of stuff you use for insulation in houses, only we paint it green. We put delicate flowers like daisies and orchids in water picks and arrange them in the polyethylene according to design. Flowers like mums we glue on with a special glue we make up called oasis. Want to know more?"

"Keep talking. I like the sound of your voice."

She pointed out a clown on the schematics. "I'll sculpt his face with pencil rod steel and then use farina paste over that. To get the black around his eyes, I'll make a paste of seaweed, it dries shiny. For red cheeks we use paprika or chili powder. For black buttons, we use onion seed."

"You could eat the damned thing."

Felicia laughed. "Not quite."

"How much does one of these babies cost a sponsor?"

"C.E. Bent and Son's floats start at a hundred thousand—"

"Dollars?"

"Of which I get five percent."

"My lord! You're rich."

"I am not. Mostly, I'm self-employed. I have to pay my own taxes, fund my own retirement—"

"You think about those things."

"If I didn't, who would? The art department throws work my way. I do side jobs, and I just picked up a design for a float in the Chinese New Year parade in San Francisco—that's how I make ends meet."

His heart sank. "You travel?"

"Sometimes. I went to Seoul, Korea, to help with the floats for the Olympics."

Harry did not pursue the subject. It was not tactful to discuss money. Practical perhaps, but not tactful. Ordinarily he was uncomfortable around women who earned more money than he did. Oddly, with Felicia he felt no discomfort whatever. He was just impressed.

"Most women as tough and smart as you have warts on their noses to warn the unsuspecting away," he said with a smile.

"You see me as tough?" She was torn between feeling happy and hurt. For once in her life she wanted to be seen as petite and feminine.

"I expect anyday now you'll be called to come bend steel on *That's Incredible*."

Agitated, Felicia rolled up her float designs. "Let's go."

Harry felt the responsibility of being a man on the verge of falling in love. "You're angry."

She gazed directly into his eyes. "I'm not angry. I just don't like men taking pot shots at me. You want some steel-bending Amazon who cuddles and coos on cue and needs taking care of—go find her."

"Do buses run out this way on Sunday?"

"I said I'd take you to pick up a paper and doughnuts and I will."

"Grudgingly," he said to her retreating back. "Hell, I'll walk, it's only twelve blocks."

"You're trying to lay a guilt trip on me. It won't work. Get in the car."

"Twist my arm."

"Please."

"Okay."

He bought his paper from a boy working a busy intersection. Then Felicia waited silently in the car with the motor running while he went in to get doughnuts.

Moments later she pulled into her parking slot, moved out of the car and slammed the door. She looked over the roof at Harry, who had done the same. "Stay away from me."

In the upstairs hall while she fumbled with her key, Harry leaned against his apartment door like a boxer spoiling for a fight. "Sure you don't want a chocolate twist?"

"No, thank you." She put a stiff coating of dignity on the exchange. "I've got work to do."

Once inside the apartment Harry tore through the paper looking for his horoscope. Just out of curiosity, he told himself.

"A simmering dispute with your mate or favorite companion can suddenly erupt if you say or do the wrong thing."

No wonder he didn't believe in astrology!

He read on: "Watch out. The other person can precipitate a flare-up. Be wary of letting your heart rule your head."

Maybe there *was* something to astrology after all!

FELICIA STOOD quite still; locked in place. This can't be happening! The sketches she had made of Harry had been ripped to shreds! Her eyes darted about the apartment, picking up the other telltale signs of intrusion. Magazines had been straightened, dirty dishes had been washed and stacked tidily on the drain board.

She braced herself and entered the bedroom. It, too, was tidy, far more so than she had left it. She backed out and ran into the hall, pounding on Harry's door.

"Harry!"

His door flew open.

She waved her arm towards her apartment. "They came again."

He yanked her inside and went into his bedroom, emerging a moment later, a gun in his right hand, held down along the side of his leg. Gone was the laid-back, smiling, enigmatic Harry she knew. In its place was a steely faced, no-nonsense, self-possessed man bent on doing justice or destruction. His eyes blazed.

"Stay here," he commanded.

Felicia swallowed, her gaze transfixed on the gun. "You might get hurt. You might hurt someone else!"

"Don't waste time! Did you see him?"

"No, but I didn't check the closet or the bathroom. Please. Be careful."

He slipped out the door and closed it quietly behind him. Felicia leaned against the wall, waiting, her senses alert to every nuance of sound. She could faintly hear music coming up from the apartment below; a horn honked, somewhere in Harry's apartment a faucet dripped. She felt as if she were in the middle of one of life's crueler jokes.

Harry returned. "Nothing and nobody. Did you leave the fire escape window open?" He put the gun in the kitchen drawer.

Felicia suddenly felt exhausted. "Yes, but not all the way, just propped open with a book. But I always have, except when I was out of town. The apartment is suffocating if I don't."

"That's pretty stupid," he said, his concern for her evident in his anger.

"But it's Sunday! There are people all around."

"You weren't. I wasn't." He led her back to her apartment. "Show me what alerted you."

She pointed to the wastepaper basket. "They tore up those sketches I made of you, washed my dishes..." She pulled him into the bedroom. "My bed is remade with the pillows under the spread. I always leave them on top."

For a single frame of time she saw Harry in her bed. Felt his touch. The quality of the memory astounded her. He had seemed to know instinctively how best to please her. Abruptly, she turned.

"Look, my jewelry box is open."

"Anything missing?"

She looked through it. "No. I don't understand this. What do these people want?"

"We'll find out."

"How?"

"First, I'll check with the other tenants. They may have seen or heard something." In less than a half hour Harry was back. "Alphonse said they weren't home. He took Mildred and Clare to see somebody named Cora—"

Felicia nodded. "She's in a nursing home recovering from a broken hip. She has the apartment across from Lila."

Harry stepped into the hall. "What about the other two apartments on our floor? I've never noticed any traffic from them."

"Cooper uses the one down from me just to store things in. Jimmy Miles has the one next to you. But he's almost never there. He's a sound technician, does free-lance work for film producers. He's off somewhere in Europe now. If he was back, we'd know it. He always alerts Mildred. She dusts and airs it for him."

"Oh? How well do you know him?"

"Well enough to know he wouldn't terrorize me. He's old enough to be my father, and gay."

"What about Ernest Ross? He seems taken with you."

"What could he hope to gain? And anyway, I can't imagine him making beds and doing dishes. Harry, isn't that peculiar?"

"It's probably someone trying to cover up the fact they've been in here and putting too fine an edge on it."

"But who? Why?"

"A crazy is who, and crazies don't need a reason other people would understand."

She leaned on the kitchen counter, cheeks cupped in her hands. "What am I going to do? Three weeks ago my life was reasonably well-ordered. Three weeks ago I thought I could cope with anything life threw at me." And whatever insecurities she had were buried deep, out of fate's way. "Then Mother died and I found out about my twin brother. Now nothing in my life seems to fit."

Harry came alert. "What did your mother leave you?"

"Hospital bills took everything. No," she said sadly, summoning in her mind the pleasant cadence of her mother's voice, her soft-eyed smile. "She left lots of nice memories."

"But suppose your twin is alive? Suppose he feels slighted or angry that—"

"What are you saying?"

"Maybe he was abandoned at birth, given up for adoption—"

"My parents would never have abandoned one of their children!"

"Don't let your temper make your decisions. I'm only raising possibilities. Parents keep a lot from their children. You'd be surprised."

"Not mine. They were as ordinary as soap."

"You won't mind if I do some checking."

"I'm sorry now I got you involved."

"I want to be involved."

It was a comment of double meaning; it captured Felicia's full attention. There was no anchor in her life now. Was that what he was offering—an anchor, a lifeline. She thought again of him lying beside her last night. She almost didn't recognize herself. She closed her eyes and shook her head.

"Don't give me that," Harry said, stumped. He had put the line out. She wasn't reeling it in. He expelled a long breath. "Well, it's been quite a weekend."

Felicia was careful not to display any visible reaction. "Yes, it has."

"Next time you go out, lock up." He wanted to reach out and touch her in some way that would convey what his words did not. But, hell, he'd probably get that wrong, too. He moved instead to leave. "That offer of a chocolate twist still stands."

"I'm not hungry."

"Call your friend Zelda, and ask her to spend the night."

"I don't need a caretaker."

"I don't think you have any idea what you need."

"Maybe I don't."

"I'll check with you when I have something on your brother."

"Thank you."

Harry entertained one last impulse to grab her, crush her in his arms, and cover her with kisses. Instead, he made the sensible decision that the timing wasn't right for either of them.

"WE ALL OUGHT to get together and ask Cooper to have the locks changed on our doors," said Mildred.

"What about putting a lock on the foyer entrance?" put in Clare.

"That wouldn't work. How would the mailman get in to put mail in our boxes? Anyway, then we'd need buzzers and an intercom system. Cooper would never go for that."

"Ernest wouldn't like that," Lila said tremulously.

"Ernest doesn't like anything," snapped Clare. Lila shrank back in the lawn chair.

Felicia stood up and forced a smile. She didn't want to appear panic-stricken. "Well, I just thought I'd check with you. I just wish I knew what they were after."

"Maybe you have something that doesn't belong to you," Lila said in a surprisingly steady voice.

Felicia shook her head. "I can't think what it would be."

"They keep cleaning up behind you. Maybe they have a dirt fetish," said Clare. "You know things like that are rooted in sex."

Mildred fixed Clare with an off-color smirk. "Trust you to come up with that."

"Well, I don't like it. We've had such a nice, quiet building for years now. Not like it was at first."

"How was it early on?" Felica asked.

"Oh, we had some doozies," Clare said, pouring herself another cup of tea. "We used to be upscale, you know. We had movie actors, kept women—"

Mildred snickered. "Clare used to try to get herself invited to tête-à-têtes. When she failed at that, she'd sit out here in the garden and get titillated watching the shades being drawn."

"That's not true!"

Mildred smiled up at Felicia. "It's true all right. Ask Cora. She was one of the kept women. She was grand in those days before age and arthritis."

Clare frowned. "She'd die if she heard you say that."

"She's not the least bit ashamed of it. Next time we go visit Cora, you should come, Felicia. She asked about you."

"Cora was a kept woman?" Lila said timidly. "That's a sin."

"There's sin and then there's sin," Mildred admonished. "Next time we go visit Cora, you can come along, too. She wants to meet you." Mildred patted Lila's hand. "And afterward, we'll all have a luncheon at the Plaza."

Clare brightened. "Your treat?"

"No, you can dip into your Wells Fargo stash. You owe me."

Felicia made a hasty retreat before she was asked to referee the battle. Halfway up the back stairs she caught sight of Harry sitting on his windowsill. She stopped.

"Nice night," he said civilly.

"Yes," she answered. In a moment's reflection she understood that Harry was still occupying some of her emptiness; that space in her that she had never been able to pin down.

An uneasy sensation about herself lingered. It was as if someone had snapped her photo and lopped off the top of her head, or an arm, a part of her that would've made the photo a complete composition—given it balance—if only the camera had been focused. That's what she needed in her life, focus and balance.

"I've moved my bed right up to the window," Harry said. "I sleep lightly. If anyone comes up this way, I'll be on top of them."

With your gun, Felicia thought, stifling a shudder. She hated the thought of violence. She paused to look at her array of plants, picked up the spray bottle and began to mist them. "I've been thinking. Isn't it odd that whoever it is always seems to know when I'm out?"

"Not so odd, just luck."

"Mine or his?"

"Both. What needs figuring is the motive."

"I have a feeling... I don't know what else to call it... I sense a—a *presence*, Zelda would say it's left-over energy."

So would my mother, Harry thought, but he decided to keep that thought to himself. "If you insist on keeping your window open, fill the space on the floor with a stack of pots and pans." *Or ask me to come over and sleep with you and I'll protect you for life. Fat chance!*

"I'll do that." She gave one last surreptitious glance at the warm nook where his jaw met his neck, then hesitated, waiting.

"Good night," he said.

So that's it, she thought. I've lost my chance with him. She stepped over the low sill into her own space—space she had once shared with Harry. It seemed a lifetime ago instead of only last night. Still, the taste and texture of him lingered in her mind.

She retrieved the torn sketches from the trash can and sorted out the pieces. None of the drawings was salvageable. She knew that. Carefully she redid a sketch; head and shoulders, hands. Working from memory, his eyes wouldn't come right.

She couldn't seem to capture the depth of their golden gleam.

Chapter Eight

"The timing has got to be lengthened," Felicia insisted to the assistant engineer in charge of overseeing the floats. His name was Grady and usually he was one of her favorite people. Today it seemed to her they were at cross purposes. "Otherwise the baby mouse runs around the mother mouse just when she makes the sweep with the broom. The baby will slam into it."

Grady's brow puckered. "That's about the hundredth thing you've found fault with this morning."

"It's my job, my float."

"Felicia—take a week off. It's early in the year, one of your floats is complete, this one is about ready to roll—"

"And, there are a half dozen other people who need to go over things with the engineer," said Patsy, one of the float designers hovering nearby.

Felicia gave her a cool glare. "I'm just staying on top of things."

"Smothering them, you mean," said Patsy. "Putting everybody in a bad mood for the rest of us. Lighten up."

Felicia looked down at her clipboard. "I'm sorry. Things seemed to be piling up on me."

Grady clucked with sympathy. "You just buried your mother, dear heart. Take some time off, a few more days won't hurt one way or another."

Felicia smiled weakly. "Maybe you're right." It was strange. Sometimes it was almost as if she had forgotten her mother was dead, and then, like now, having it mentioned—it would hit her all over again, the grief and the aching sense of loss, as vivid and agonizing as ever.

Grady continued clucking. "If we run into a problem, I'll call you. By next Monday, we'll have this float ready for final check—the polyethylene will be ready for painting."

At the end of the work day indecision and grief followed Felicia home and hung there while she made a cautious entry into her apartment. She put indecision and grief aside. She had a more involved ritual now. She examined the contents of drawers she had left just so, the closet with shoes deliberately mismatched and misaligned.

Discovering all remained as she had arranged it, she opened the windows to the evening breeze that swept down off Mount Wilson.

Standing there with the breeze kissing her cheeks, she cocked her head, listening for activity from Harry's apartment. She heard none.

She returned to the living room and called Zelda. "You weren't at work today."

"I had arrangements to make."

"What arrangement? Did your romantic interlude come off?"

"Almost. I got invited to a wedding—in Texas. Aunt Evelyn called me. My cousin is getting married. The best man is single."

"You're going to Texas? Just like that?"

"It's not 'just like that.' My astrology transit said I'd be taking a trip. I've known it for weeks. You won't miss me, you have Harry to occupy you."

"What does he have to do with this?"

"Everything. When I find the man who's right for me, do you think I'd dump it all on you? Of course not."

"Harry's not right for me. All we do is fight."

"You and Harry could've been married in a past life. Your arguments might be the spiritual residue of that."

"I didn't call you to talk about Harry or past lives."

"Oh? Why did you call?"

Felicia bit her tongue. "When're you leaving?"

"Well . . . nine-forty tonight looks good. Otherwise the next favorable window of travel is three days from now. If I wait until then I'd miss some of the fun bridal showers."

"What about work?"

"Nothing about it. I don't have any extra jobs in right now. Grady's keeping an eye on my floats. Things are pretty well caught up. By the way, I called Thea and gave her your address. She can explain anything you don't understand about your chart when you get it. Ask her about Harry—"

"You have Harry on the brain."

"So do you, if only you'd admit it. I've got to finish packing. I'll send you a card. Ta."

Felicia cradled the phone and curled up on the sofa. She gazed at the ceiling, staring at the cracks. She tried to impose the path her life was taking along the seams that split and turned back upon themselves. She gave it up as a lost cause and went to the fridge. She had always been one of those lucky souls who could feed her misery and never gain an ounce. Pork chops, hamburger, baked potato? Nothing held enough appeal to warrant cooking it.

She settled for an orange and went to sit on the fire escape, peeling it and disposing of the rind in an empty flowerpot.

The evening sky was dull and cloudy. Not at all what a late-spring night should be like. But she had lived in Pasadena long enough to know that the threat of rain was usually just that, a threat with no substance. Nevertheless, Clare and Mildred must be taking it seriously. There was no tea-time hustle and bustle about the garden. Felicia sighed. She longed for someone to talk to—or listen to. She felt the weight of her mother's absence. If she could have her back only for an instant! Just long enough to clear up the mystery of her twin. That'd be all she'd ask.

She glanced over at Harry's window. Solidly closed.

Her hands were sticky with the sweetness of the orange. She went in to wash them. Sinking deeper into her reflective mood she looked up the number of the cemetery sexton. When he came on the line, she was certain she'd interrupted his dinner.

"It's Felicia Bennington," she told him.

"Who?"

"My mother was buried at Wildwood Gardens a few weeks ago...Winifred Bennington."

He made no attempt to hide his dismay. "You've called before."

"That's right. I was checking to see if you by any chance had a record of my brother being buried there—"

"I recall I told you, no."

"I—could you check again? For an infant, Thomas Adam Bennington. The records would be almost thirty years old by now."

"Thirty or sixty, don't make no nevermind. There ain't no Thomas Adam Bennington, infant, buried in Wildwood, not in your family plot—nor anywheres else."

Felicia hated to let the hope go, but no choice was offered. "I'm sorry I disturbed you again. I just felt the need to be certain."

He relented. "We get calls like this all the time. Sorry about your mother, miss."

Felicia gently cradled the receiver. "Me, too," she said to herself.

She turned the television on low for company, lay down on the sofa and fought her confusion and sense of futility with imaginary scenes. She saw herself poring through the sexton's records and finding a scrap of paper that had somehow been overlooked, detailing Thomas Adam's burial. She scoured the cemetery until she found a tiny headstone of carved angels beneath which she placed a lovely bouquet of white flowers.

Her mind's eye drifted. She arrived home and caught red-handed the culprit who was invading her privacy. She was strong and wonderfully effective. She knocked him down and held him until Harry came running with his gun.

Then she and Harry... Felicia erased that picture before it was well drawn in her mind. There were only so many things a person could worry about at any one time.

The thudding in the hall brought her upright. It came again, as if someone were shoving against her door. A slow sharp edge of terror spliced up her spine. It couldn't be the intruder—could it? Did he think she wasn't at home?

Noise. She needed to make some noise. She reached out and turned the television volume as high as it would go. The sudden squall of a game show filled the apartment.

The thudding became more pronounced.

Someone was yelling.

She put her ear up to the door. Damn Cooper. He should at least give them peep holes. The thudding came again, the door vibrated with it.

"Who's out there!"

Muttering. She thought she caught her name. Quietly, she turned the knob, opening the door a crack. Harry stood there, keys held between his teeth, his arms laden, the bags balanced beneath his chin. He raised an eyebrow at her, then spat the keys out. They landed with a thunk on the floor. "What the hell is going on in there?"

Felicia unlatched the safety chain, allowed him in, went to turn off the television, then swung around. She felt shaky, her knees weak, and a nerve was jumping at the base of her throat. "You scared me."

"What do you think you did to me? I knocked and all hell broke loose."

"I turned the TV up. I thought if they knew I was home, they'd go away."

"They?"

"Whoever it is who keeps coming in here!"

His expression hardened. "They came again? Today?"

"No—I wasn't taking any chances."

"Good girl," he said approvingly. He began unloading parcels onto the kitchen counter. A manila file folder slid from beneath his arm, falling, its contents scattering. Felicia bent to pick it up. Harry grabbed her arm and jerked her away. "I'll get those."

He scooped up the photographs, turning them away from her eyes and shuffling them back into the manila folder. He placed the folder at the far end of the counter.

"Why so secretive?" Then she thought she knew. "Those have something to do with my brother."

"Not a chance. They're from an old L.A. County case, for my thesis. And one look at them would ruin your appetite." He grinned, indicating the parcels he'd unloaded. "You do have an appetite? Just in case it's finicky, I've got egg rolls, fried rice, hot spiced chicken, fried chicken, mashed potatoes—"

"I don't recall that we were planning to have dinner together tonight." Even as she said it she realized that she was so happy to see him, she would've accepted a dinner of mud pies.

"It's a spur-of-the-moment thing."

She couldn't just let him take charge of her life. "Your spur," she said.

His eyes took her in and settled her near his heart. "Our moment."

"Suppose I'm busy? Or have a date?"

He froze, afraid his peace gesture and good intentions were going down the drain. "Do you?"

"No."

"Then humor me. I have some news for you. I checked out Thomas Adam today."

Felicia's breath caught in her throat. "Tell me."

He began opening the cartons of food. "After dinner."

"That's blackmail." Though taut, there wasn't a bit of sarcasm or anger in her voice. Despite her words, she was glad to see him again. And the last thing she wanted to do was start an argument and have him stalk out without telling her what he'd discovered. "Shall we have white wine or hot tea?" she asked.

He reached into a bag and brought out a small bottle of sake. "How about heating this up? Later, we can have coffee."

"You've thought of everything."

"I got tired of crying for the moon, thought I'd take a little action and see where it got me."

"Where is that?"

He looked at her, his amber eyes alight with enchanting golden flecks. "Why, right here, sweetheart. Right here."

They ate off the coffee table sitting on sofa cushions on the floor with the lights dimmed; Felicia lighted vanilla-scented candles. She sipped warmed rice wine sparingly, it made her light-headed and loosened her tongue. The candlelight contrived to soften even Harry's appearance. He was aglow. Her senses were pleasantly sharpened and she countered his gentle teasing and banter with some of her own.

Harry sensed she was keeping a sentry on her feelings. He could tell she'd stick to her guns, not letting him take charge of her. And he admired her for it. Still, what he wanted to do was find himself magically beside her again, caressing the curve of her neck. Finally, satiated with food, he leaned his back against the sofa. "In all the state of California there isn't a death certificate for a Thomas Adam Bennington."

"That's not possible—it simply is *not* possible," she said, realizing she'd built up her own expectations too far.

"He's not dead in California—or Oregon, or any of the bordering states. Which raises the distinct possibility that your brother is alive and well—"

"Not well. It says so on the birth certificate. He was handicapped in some way."

"Then search for him among the handicapped."

"Among...?"

"Places... Listen, one of the guys on the force had a daughter who was born with serious brain damage. She was a vegetable. He and his wife kept her at home until she was about seven. Then they put her in an institution. They had to. It became too expensive to keep her at home. She had to have a special breathing apparatus, she got sick all the time. He was always having to rush home or to the hospital. He couldn't keep his mind on work, his marriage was falling apart. They focused so on the daughter, his older son felt left out, started doing drugs..."

"That's cruel. My parents wouldn't set aside a baby. They wouldn't. They were warm and caring... loving."

"So is my friend on the force. Were your parents wealthy? Could they have afforded round-the-clock care? Machines, special equipment? I haven't been out of the hospital so long myself, y'know. You should see the bills. Luckily, insurance covered most of it. Thirty years ago there was no such thing as Medicare and Medicaid. So think! What would your parents have done!"

"You make a convincing argument. My brother— alive?"

"Why not?"

"Mother would've told me."

"Maybe she planned to. What'd she die of?"

Felicia's face fell. "Brain tumor...she seldom knew me at the end."

"She didn't have control of her faculties."

Felicia shook her head.

"Ask yourself this question. If your brother *is* alive—do you want to find him. You may be opening up a can of worms."

"Of course I want to find him!"

"Don't go hostile on me—I'm playing devil's advocate."

"I appreciate it. Really. So, what should I do?"

"Write letters—no—compose one letter and have it printed up—you'll need hundreds of copies. Then start mailing them out to full-care centers around the state. Start with the ones in your home county. Try the hospitals first, they transfer patients to all kinds of special interest facilities. Explain what you're doing. You may get better results if you use a white lie when you ask them to check their records."

"What white lie?"

"Say that you're searching for your brother so that your parent's estate can be settled. Everybody dreams that some lost relative will die and leave them a windfall."

"You make it sound so simple."

"It's a variation on a common police investigative procedure. What you'd be doing is throwing out a net and hoping to pull in some information."

"You've given this a lot of thought."

He grinned. "My brain works in mysterious ways. Would that I could solve my own problems so simply."

"What problems?"

"How to keep on your good side, for one."

"You do all right."

"You think so?"

"Name your other problems."

"Well, I'm trying to figure out how I can write a thesis that my professor can't skim for an article under his own name, and still get a passing grade. This is the last thing I need for my degree. By the way, that's what those photos are for. He specifically requested photos."

"But you said they'd ruin my appetite."

"They're gory. I'm thinking no publication would print them."

"You can always put a copyright symbol on your thesis. That way he couldn't use any part of it without giving you credit."

"He could and would. The man has no scruples."

"But, you'd have your degree by then?"

"Sure..."

"Then contact the same magazines he would and offer to do the articles yourself."

Harry paused, thinking. "But, I can't write."

"You do briefs don't you?"

"Yes, but they aren't the same thing."

"Do the magazines pay for these articles?"

"Hell, yes. If they didn't Professor Lawson wouldn't waste his time—and my research. He doesn't just publish in law journals."

Felicia gave him her most alluring smile. "Harry...when it comes to preventing injustice, like this slimy professor getting money and credit for your work, you can do anything."

He grinned back. "You have a point."

"There's another point. Even if Lawson does write an article and gets it published, all you have to do is remind the publisher of your letter, send proof that the article was based on your research without your permission and insist they send you a check in the same amount they paid Lawson. If nothing else, it would make them pause the next time Lawson submitted something."

"I like that. I like it very much." He met her eyes. "I like you."

Every nerve ending in Felicia's body tingled. Excitement stirred in the pit of her stomach. She had a great deal to be grateful to Harry for. He had been on hand to get her out of trouble when she needed him. But *like*? She saw him as more than a friend. She had never in her life gone to bed with just a friend. She rose gracefully from the cushion. "Why don't I make coffee now?"

Harry shrugged. "Yes, why don't you?"

While she was in the kitchen he returned the cushions to the sofa, gathered up the debris from the coffee table and disposed of it. There was still one topic they had not touched upon in depth. "About your mysterious gremlin—" he began, turning toward the kitchen. Felicia was standing at the end of the counter, her expression reflected her shock as she examined the contents of the manila folder. "Damn it!" he yelled. "I told you not to look at those!"

Her eyes were out of focus. "I didn't mean to. It's horrible." The pictures were etched in her mind, never to be erased, she was certain. In color, garish, impersonal, the remains of what had once been a man, a severed head, the eyes open and seeming to stare up at her—all seeing. "Do people really do this to one another?"

He closed the folder and put his arms around her. "All the time."

"How can you stay so...so normal after seeing things like that?" She was trying to imagine what it must be like, understand his other dimensions, curious as to how he inured himself to such horror.

"Some of us don't." With his arm about her shoulders he led her to the sofa. "You need a glass of water? A drink?"

"I couldn't swallow." In fact, her stomach felt queasy. She feared she was going to be sick. He didn't release her, but kept his arms about her.

"Take a deep breath," he said. It was in his mind that he had to do something, get her mind off the photos. He watched her inhale, exhale, noted when color began returning to her face, when the telltale white began to disappear from around her mouth. "Better?"

"Much. Thanks." His fingers tightened, drawing her closer. She could feel his nearness through every pore in her body. Then his lips were on hers and she was no longer thinking, only feeling.

After a long moment he pulled away. She opened her eyes to see him looking down at her, his expression masked by shadows. His eyes hypnotized her; everything in her was stilled and waiting, every muscle, ever nerve.

"I know where I'd like this to take us," he said softly. He knew he meant more than bed, and hoped what he said made sense to her.

She leaned her head against his broad chest, breathing in the heady man-scent of him. It was pure insanity, she thought, but it felt wonderful to be in his arms, wonderful to be wanted. It was as if she had two brains in her head, one watching the other, guiding it, telling it to let go. Deep within her all her emptiness ached with need. She took his hand and led him into the bedroom.

"YOU'RE AWFULLY QUIET," he observed.

They were propped against the headboard, not touching, sipping the coffee she'd perked hours earlier. Now and again the moon came out from beneath a cloud and sent shafts of pale light into the room.

"I was just thinking how much my life has changed."

"Since you met me?"

"That's a fair statement—maybe even understated."

"You having regrets?"

"I'm curious about where we're headed."

"Where do you think?" he said warily. He knew he was afraid of falling in love. It was a painful process. He felt weak, more vulnerable now than when he'd been laid up in the hospital while others saw to his most basic, simplest needs. He wasn't about to stick his neck out, have it chopped off for a fool. If she said it first, he'd say it too.

She heard the caution in his voice and sought for her own cautious words. "I don't know, you're a much nicer person than I first thought."

"Nicer? *Nicer!*" He muttered an expletive. "Nice guys finish last."

"That's a cliché." She cocked her head. "What was that sound?"

"My heart beating, or trying to."

"Don't joke." She put her coffee cup on the bed-side table. "Listen," she whispered. "Somebody is on the fire escape."

"I didn't hear anything, but I'll check." He felt around and found his underwear.

The moon went behind clouds again, its trail of light fading. Felicia held herself motionless. "Hurry," she murmured.

Harry slipped around the bed and sidled up to the open window. He heard plants rustling. What was it—someone standing there watching him?

"Boo!" he shouted.

"Arrrgh!"

"Lights!" Harry shouted.

Felicia grabbed for the lamp, snapped it on.

Harry grabbed the shadowy figure and yanked it over the sill.

Felicia gasped, "Alphonse!" and pulled the bed sheet up to her chin.

Harry helped the old man to his feet. "What the hell were you doing?"

His face flushed, Alphonse gathered his robe and dignity about himself. "There...uh...there was an unusual amount of noise from Felicia's bedroom. Mine is just below. I'm sorry m'dear," he said, addressing Felicia as if across an elegantly laid dining table. "What with all the trouble you've been experiencing, I thought perhaps you needed help. I was imagining all sorts of evil." He turned back to Harry. "Sorry, old boy. Didn't mean to interrupt. I'll just go out the way I came, shall I?"

He stepped over the sill and back into the night. "It's just Harry," he called on his way downstairs.

Mildred's voice floated up. "Put that hoe down, Clare. The excitement's over."

The voices mingled, then faded, doors slammed. Harry looked at Felicia. Her cheeks were aflame. "Now, don't get mad at me."

"If you hadn't dropped your shoes like bricks—"

"It wasn't my shoes. The bed squeaks."

"Because you want to do acrobatics."

"Oh, so now it's all my fault an old crock peeps in your window!" He began tugging on his jeans.

"Alphonse is not an old crock." Her eyes widened. "You're not . . ."

He nodded. "I have to deliver subpoenas at the crack of dawn. If I stay I'll only wake you up when I leave." He sat beside her on the bed and bent to kiss her on the forehead. "And we probably wouldn't get a wink of sleep. Will you consider that we've had our obligatory tiff and made up already? Or shall we make up later? We're getting awfully good at making up. By the way, do you know that even rumpled you are very lovely?"

"Thank you," she said, halfway suspicious of his sudden willingness to pitch himself headlong into a romance. But she warmed with pleasure because, cautious or not, he was making an oblique reference to their future.

He bundled up his shoes and shirt. "Lock the door behind me."

Sheet dragging, Felicia trailed him to the door.

She lay awake the remainder of the night filled with a deep cold loneliness mingled with a growing sense of excitement about Harry.

The scent of him lingered in the bed linens. She told herself it was her usual pattern: initial burst of interest, the ritualistic courtship, a sense of something special happening—and finally—the ultimate disappointment.

The only thing was, Harry didn't disappoint her. He made her feel wonderful, as if she belonged, as if with him she could face the world and conquer it.

Chapter Nine

Writing letters was anathema to her. It was so much easier to reach for the telephone. But this letter, an appeal to find something, anything about her twin drove Felicia to her computer. She agonized over the composition, edited and rewrote. Once finished, she still had to find out where to send it. Would anyone recall a baby boy who had been in their care almost thirty years ago?

At the library she discovered a directory of nursing homes, hospitals, convalescent centers listed by state and city. The directory was thick, the list seemed endless. She had the letter run off at a copy shop and bought two hundred envelopes, fearful lest she miss the one hospital or nursing home that had information about Thomas Adam Bennington. In the afternoon she addressed envelopes until her fingers cramped.

Her mind was not entirely on this task. She kept her door open and an ear cocked for the sound of Harry's footsteps in the hall.

She had in mind to offer him dinner. Fried chicken, baked potatoes. They'd talk. A relationship could not survive without friendship. And this time she would not allow a hostile thought or word to pass her lips.

A sense of purpose flooded her veins.

She took a chicken out of the freezer to defrost, washed and oiled two potatoes, arrange the small table for two with candles. The table setting looked sparse. It required a piece of greenery, a sprig of flowers.

She heard the commotion in the garden before she stepped to the fire escape. Voices being raised in anger.

Against a backdrop of blooming purple jacaranda Clare and Mildred were presenting themselves as a united front to Ernest. Behind them, Lila huddled, eyes pinched closed, wringing her hands.

Felicia hesitated, it wasn't any of her business. This rationalization was immediately erased with a rush of guilt. Clare and Mildred had been surrogate mothers to her, interested in her life, her career; even if they were also overbearing, quick to criticize and too nosy by far.

The sight of Lila, so obviously frightened, tugged at her. Clare and Mildred seemed a mild defense in the face of Ernest yelling and waving his arms. He looked puffed up like a blowfish, and ready to explode.

She had to join the fray on the side of justice. "What's going on?" she asked.

Clare spun about. "Ernest is trying to force Lila into a nursing home," she cried. "Make him listen to reason."

Felicia heard the fear in Clare's voice, recognizing it for what it was: if it could happen to Lila, it could happen to Clare, who was fifteen years Lila's senior.

"I'm not forcing Mother to do anything," Ernest said in a voice dripping with unction. "I merely want her to see a doctor. She's talking to herself—"

"Everyone does that," snorted Mildred. "It doesn't mean we're ready for a straitjacket."

Lila's face was thick with makeup, her lipstick garish, the mascara smeared down tear tracks. Felicia took her arm. "Are you feeling okay?"

Her touch seemed to strike some chord in Lila. The older woman twisted violently out of her grasp. "I'm not crazy! Ernest wants me to be crazy. He thinks I don't know things, but I do. He doesn't like me. He won't bring my grandchildren to see me and he won't let me go anywhere."

"They're teenagers," Ernest sputtered. "I can't make them come here. I can't even get them to the dinner table!" He gestured helplessly to Clare and Mildred, gave Felicia a pained smile. "Ladies, this is none of your affair. Allow me to speak to my mother alone."

"Wouldn't it be better to wait until Lila has calmed down," Felicia put in. "She's—"

"I'm Mother's guardian," he said warningly. "I can call an attorney."

"Bully!" Mildred accused.

"I pay Mother's rent, I look after her. I'm responsible for her. She isn't taking care of herself—she's stopped taking her medicine."

"Ernest wants me to go where I can't take my birds," Lila said, whimpering. "He wants me to write my name on papers. I don't want to write my name."

Felicia turned back to Ernest. "What kind of papers?"

"Not that it's any of your business, but Mother owns a piece of property. I'm selling it to meet her expenses. I need her power of attorney."

Felicia paused, thinking. "Wouldn't you already have that if you're her guardian?"

Ernest's little mustache twitched. His eyes narrowed to slits. "These matters are involved," he said condescendingly.

Lila continued to whimper.

Mildred put her arms around Lila and glared at Ernest. "Look what you've done. You ought to be ashamed. Go away or we'll call somebody..."

"We'll call the newspaper," Clare said. "And tell them you're abusing Lila, that's what we'll do."

Ernest muttered an oath. "You crazy old broad, you don't have the right to interfere."

"You couldn't bear up under the scandal, could you?" Clare threw out, chins wavering. "Big-shot realtor trying to take his mother to the cleaners, that's you. Your name would be mud in the fancy community you live in. I've met your kind before."

A pallor fell across Ernest's face. For a fleeting moment he almost looked scared—but it was so fleeting Felicia discounted what she'd seen.

"What medicine does Lila take?" she asked. "We could remind her—"

"That won't be necessary," he snapped. The look he gave Lila was not that of a loving son. "You're overstepping yourself by trying to influence Mother against me. I warn you, if she's found wandering the streets she'll put herself in a hospital, or—" He didn't finish the sentence, but allowed the threat to hang in the air.

Mildred's narrow shoulders stiffened. "In this building we look after our own. Go away. Old broad, indeed. You have no respect."

"Maybe if you give it a couple of days..." Felicia suggested, trying to be conciliatory.

"The law is on my side," he insisted.

"We're on Lila's side," Clare said. "We won't let you take her."

It was a standoff, recognized by all—no losers, no winners.

Ernest threw up his hands. The diamond pinky ring he wore flashed in the sun.

"I'll be back, ladies. You want trouble, I'll give you trouble."

Lila brushed a cloud of gray hair out of her eyes. "I have to feed Tweetie Birds...I have to watch—" She stopped and looked hard at Felicia. "I don't like you. I know I don't." Her face was suddenly creased with alarm. "You—"

"There, there," Mildred crooned. "You're just upset, dear. Felicia is as much your friend as we are. Here, sit down while I go make us a pot of tea. I have a packet of that Earl Grey you like. Alphonse will be along in a bit and we'll ask him what's best to do."

At the back door Ernest collided with Harry, but kept on going.

"What the hell—?"

Harry's head was wrapped with gauze, his shirt torn and bloody, and as he approached, Felicia noticed he was limping worse than usual. Mildred and Clare began to cluck around him like mother hens.

Felicia hung back but she felt her heart leap to her throat. "You wrecked your car," she said.

"Nope. I served a subpoena to a very nasty individual." He thumbed in the direction of Ernest's retreating back. "What was that all about?"

"That bully," said Mildred. "He's trying to force Lila to sign away her property. Next thing you know, he'll have her in a nursing home, certain. He said she's talking to herself. As if that makes a person nutty."

Felicia had eyes only for Harry. "Are you badly hurt?"

He started to say no, looked at Felicia and changed his mind. "I might have a concussion."

"You ought to be in bed," urged Clare. She giggled. "Your own bed."

"I am a bit dizzy." He watched Felicia out of the corner of his eye and decided to play his injuries for all they were worth. He swayed.

Felicia stepped away from the garden table. "Let me help you upstairs before you fall down," she said, reaching to slip an arm around his waist and guide him indoors.

"All this fighting and arguing..." Clare sighed. "I wish Alphonse had been here. He would've routed Ernest in fine fashion."

"We did nicely on our own," Mildred said. "Now where did Lila get off to? Poor thing. We need to teach her to be more assertive. If she would just once stand up to Ernest."

SADIE HAD the meat cleaver and was sending it slamming into Felicia's chicken. Lila shuddered, but she couldn't stop Sadie. "Let's get out of here, Sadie. Ernest will be back. He always comes back."

"This is what she deserves! This is what Ernest deserves. I saw the way they looked at each other. She's not satisfied that she had Percy. Oh, no! Now it's Ernest. And last night she was in bed with Harry. Clare said so. You see how immoral she is. Trash. Any man will do.''

Lila felt frightened, nauseous. ''But we don't care about that you said. We only want my necklace. You should never have put on all that makeup, Sadie. Ernest knows about us. He knows.''

Lila took the cleaver, washed it and put it away. She couldn't make herself touch the pile of mangled raw chicken. ''Let's go see Tweetie Birds.''

''You're weak, Lila. Weak. Limp as wet noodles. You let Ernest walk all over you. Next time he comes, I'll handle him. You saw how scared he got when Mildred mentioned scandal.''

''Please, Sadie. Let's go.''

''Twiddle-twaddle,'' Sadie scorned, ''that's you.''

''Clare will be serving tea and maybe those little cakes I like.''

Sadie scoffed. ''Look at you! Mascara running down your face. You don't even know how to keep yourself decent anymore. And you smell like death.''

Lila cried. ''I don't. You cut up the chicken, not me.''

''Hah! You think anyone will believe that? Did Papa ever believe it was me?''

''Oh, Sadie. Why are you so mean to me? You used to be my best friend.''

Felicia stopped through the door and stopped just short of the kitchen counter. ''Lila!''

The woman spun about, her eyes alight with fear, her mouth working. Her gaze darted from Felicia to Harry. ''I didn't do it,'' she trilled in a strangely anguished tone. ''I didn't do it.''

"Lila," Felicia said, speaking softly in the face of the older woman's emerging hysteria. "No one is accusing you of anything. Why don't you come sit down." Even more softly she urged Harry to go get Mildred.

"You can't keep me here," Lila said, taking a faltering step forward.

Sadie took over. She engaged Felicia's eye, glaring at her. Head held high, Lila sauntered out the door and down the stairs.

Concerned, Felicia followed behind and leaned over the bannister. When Mildred arrived, hard on Harry's heels, she pointed to Lila's door. "She went into her own apartment," she whispered.

Mildred nodded. "I'll look in on her."

HARRY INSPECTED the chicken. It had been skillfully dissected. "I buy chicken already cut up myself. And cooked."

Exasperation coloring every gesture, Felicia washed the chicken parts, dried them and dumped them into a paper sack of flour. "You're not taking any of this seriously. Suppose it was your mother—"

"Listen, the guy may not be the apple of his mother's eye, but apparently he has the legal right—"

"Just because he said so doesn't make it so."

"I thought I was invited to a friendly dinner. To get to know each other better." The kind of knowing that interested him would take years, but Felicia didn't seem amenable to subject changes or suggestions at the moment. "You don't sound so friendly to me."

She tossed her head. "I'm friendly. I can't see Lila doing this," she went on. "Can you? What would be the point? Unless—" She paused, thoughtful. "Harry, suppose Ernest is the one who's been vandalizing me?''

"Farfetched. He's the boardroom type, steal you blind.''

"That's it!''

"It is?'' He put an arm around her, pressed his lips to the back of her neck. "Clear up the mystery for me.''

"I'm warning you,'' she said, sidestepping out of his reach. "I won't tolerate *your* being condescending.''

Harry sighed. "All right. As my captain used to say, 'Give me a motive and make it stick.'''

"That's easy. Ernest wants Lila's money.''

"She has money?''

"Apparently. Property anyway. That translates to money. He was trying to get her to sign a power of attorney so he could sell it.''

"Can you connect your gremlin to the power of attorney?''

"Easy. Ernest trashes my apartment, planning to get it blamed on Lila so that he can have her declared incompetent. She learns what he's up to and cleans up behind him to protect herself.''

He didn't want to be the one tell her how amateurish that sounded. "You really believe the guy would do something like that to his own mother?''

Felicia refused to be swayed. "Greed is a motive, isn't it? What's going on here is obviously the work of two people.''

"If you feel sure, call the police.''

"You are the police.''

"I used to be, not anymore.''

"Calling the police would work right into Ernest's hands. He'd deny he has so much as stepped foot on the second floor, let alone in my apartment. That would leave Lila. Did you see how frightened she was?"

"The woman is not right in the head—"

Felicia turned cold. "She's just scared. You have no compassion."

"Compassion is what got my legs shot out from under me," he said resolutely. "Hell, I know all about compassion—the hard kind. Giving mouth-to-mouth to some kid who's overdosed on drugs; comforting hysterical mothers at the scene of accidents; telling parents that their daughter has been found murdered and raped."

His outburst hung between them.

Felicia swallowed. "I'm sorry."

"Forget it."

"I don't want to forget it. You don't look—"

"You fell into that old adage of judging a book by its cover."

She smiled. "You're a lot like the floats I design. They look wonderfully simple from the outside, but all the complexities and working parts are beneath the surface."

"Dare I believe my ears? Was that a compliment?"

"Yes, and well deserved." She took a breath. "Now, about Lila—"

"One step forward, two backward," he said with mock seriousness. "Tell me, are you really a float designer or a social worker?"

"Ask me that when you're eighty and you need help."

"Will I still know you then?" He was teasing, but not completely.

She shot a vexed glare at him, then concentrated on pouring oil into the frying pan and setting it to warming. "Will you at least consider that it might be Ernest trying to trap his mother into being declared incompetent?"

Harry moaned inwardly. The chicken dinner she'd promised was beginning to seem a lot like crow. "I'll consider it because you seem to have a one-track mind."

"Can we prove it?"

He looked at her—dark hair framing creamy white skin, large eyes, mouth ready to smile. Her expression was serious and her imagination was all out of whack. He hated to disappoint her. "You don't have anything that would stand up in court."

"I don't want to prove anything in court. I just want to get to the bottom of this and I want my privacy intact. It gives me the shudders to think of Ernest creeping around, handling my things."

Harry didn't like that idea, either. He was feeling very protective of Felicia.

She went quiet for a heartbeat. "He's lucky to still have his mother."

Harry's eyes locked on to the throbbing vein in her slender neck. "I'm not sure I'd go along with your scenario," he said cautiously.

"What's wrong with it?"

"We found Lila in your kitchen, not Ernest. That's the fact."

"But he could've just left! Harry, pretend this is a crime scene. Investigate it."

"Nothing to investigate. You're cooking the evidence."

"I say Ernest timed his escape just right."

Harry shook his head, accidently dislodging the gauze so that his wound was visible. "You're projecting, Felicia, building a case out of thin air."

Felicia stared at the small strip of adhesive on his forehead. She moved closer for a better inspection. "That's hardly a scratch!"

He cleared his throat. "It bled a lot. I told you it wasn't bad."

"You said you had a concussion."

"I said I might have a concussion."

She glowered. "You've been playing on my sympathies! Lying. For all I know, it could've been you who came in here and sliced up this chicken. I wouldn't cook you dinner if you were starving to death."

Harry unwound the gauze from his head. "I am starving. I missed breakfast and lunch. I sat in the emergency room two hours waiting to get patched up. I admit it. I overdramatized the cut."

"Why?"

"I like the attention?"

For a moment she was angry, then she was seeing the little boy in him. Then the little boy was gone and he was very much grown up. She remembered her promise not to get angry with him tonight. She gave him a tiny smile. "You got plenty of attention."

"Tell you what—feed me and I'll do the dishes."

"What will that prove?"

"That I'm the kind of man who doesn't mind helping out around the house? Isn't that one of the requisites of today's woman?"

"I thought today's woman wasn't your kind of woman."

"That was before I met you."

"Went to bed with me, you mean."

"Hold it! I didn't bring sex into this. I can take it or leave it. If you weren't a woman with old-fashioned traits, I'd be out of here like a shot."

"Old-fashioned? I ought to feed you dinner just to hear what you'll say next."

"I don't mean in looks. I'm talking about the way you conduct yourself—"

Felicia feigned annoyance. "Oh? How is that?"

Harry searched for words. "With...elegance and modesty," he said, adding, "You're smart, too. I like that in a woman."

"Is that something else you've changed your mind about?"

He eyed the delicious-smelling chicken frying in the pan. "I've got my back against the wall in a no-win situation. Would you consider just letting me have a drumstick to take home?"

Someone knocked on the door. "Could you answer it?" she asked. "My hands are covered in flour."

"We thought we'd find you here," said Clare to Harry without innuendo. Behind her stood Mildred and Alphonse. They crowded in and stood silently for a minute, then they all began speaking at once.

Harry held up his hand.

"Alphonse, you do it," said Clare.

"You're a lawyer, Harry, we want your advice."

He balked. "I'm not a lawyer yet."

"Just say you'll help," pleaded Clare.

"I'll listen." I'm letting himself in for it, he thought.

"We look after one another," said Alphonse. "We're concerned for Lila. We think Ernest is up to something."

"So do we!" said Felicia, and over Harry's protests, she told the elders what she believed.

"We don't need caseworkers and the police snooping around, poking their noses into our business," said Mildred. "Even if Lila is a little off, so what? We can keep an eye on her. She's certainly no more eccentric than the flirtatious fossil I take care of."

"You don't take care of me," protested Clare huffily. "And, the least you could do is save that kind of talk for behind my back."

"I was just trying to make a point. Felicia, Ernest may be trying to provoke you into calling the police on Lila. Then he'd have a wonderful excuse for putting her away."

Felicia turned toward Harry. "See? I'm not the only one who came up with that idea."

"Have you noticed how Ernest has been Johnny-on-the-spot every time Felicia has had a break in?" Alphonse put in. "And I think we should keep Cooper in mind, too. If he thinks Lila's causing problems in the building, he'll evict her."

Clare nodded vigorously. "That would work right into Ernest's plot."

"Let me play devil's advocate," Harry suggested. "Why pick on Felicia?"

"That's easy. Felicia works. She's out more than the rest of us."

"What we thought," declared Mildred, "is that we'd set a trap for Ernest."

"What kind of trap?" Harry asked warily.

"We thought you'd know," said Clare.

"My idea," said Mildred, "is to catch Ernest in Felicia's apartment. Then you could—"

"No traps." Harry was adamant. "Playing amateur sleuth is one thing, but putting Felicia in harm's way is reckless. No way. Somebody could get hurt."

"We aren't amateurs," sniffed Clare. "Alphonse used to work for Pinkerton's."

Alphonse shot his cuffs. "I didn't solve every case, you'll recall. I still don't know where you hid the money you took."

Clare batted her lashes. "I'd be glad to trade the information."

Mildred made a noise in her throat. "Stop it! The issue here is Lila."

Alphonse held up a liver-spotted hand. "It seems to me Ernest is the one trying to set the trap. Suppose we just ignore what he does. Pretend like we don't have the slightest idea what's happening. Ernest would have to give up on it eventually or expose himself. Lila obviously thinks she's got things well in hand. Why don't we allow her to go on believing it?"

"We ought to tell her," said Clare. "That way she'll know we support her."

"Nix that," said Mildred. "Lila is gullible, she's liable to mention it, then Ernest will find another way to get her carted off to who-knows-where. Let's face it—Lila *is* a bit shaky. I agree with Alphonse, up to now, outside the aggravation she's caused Felicia, she's had things well in hand. It would build Lila's confidence to think she's successfully outwitting Ernest."

"I don't like any of this," Harry said. "You're absolving Lila of complicity without having a shred of evidence to do so. Felicia's safety is at stake here."

"No, it isn't," she contradicted from the kitchen. "Looking back on it, I've never been personally threatened."

"Things like this have a way of escalating," he warned. "For the sake of argument, let's say Ernest is the culprit—how did he and Lila get in your apartment today? We would've noticed them going up the fire escape."

"Oh..." Felicia poked the frying chicken with a fork. "I left my apartment door open—" She stopped in mid-sentence.

"Open," Harry prompted. "Why?"

Her chin went up. "I was watching for you."

He basked in the significance of that. "You missed me." His voice sounded like a caress.

Mildred rolled her eyes. "This is pressing the limits of virtue. Let's go."

"You're the one to know," snapped Clare. "You mangled the limits of virtue often enough."

"Never in front of others."

Clare skewered her with a look. "The way you dress up hypocrisy as moral superiority you ought to call yourself *Saint* Mildred."

Alphonse, the eternal mediator, broke in. "We've settled the issue, then? We're agreed that we just go on as before, except that we keep a keen eye on Lila."

"You're asking for trouble," said Harry.

The others overruled him.

Felicia saw the oldsters out.

"Two ex-cons, a retired Pinkerton detective and a loonie—some neighborhood we've got here," Harry said.

Felicia smiled at him, all sweetness and insouciance. "Light the candles, Harry."

"A cozy romantic dinner—just the ticket," he said, relieved.

They settled down to dinner and afterward, to his dismay, Felicia held him to his offer. While he washed dishes she finished addressing envelopes.

"What are you going to do if those don't get any response?" he asked.

"I don't know. I just know I have to do it. Anyway it makes me feel better to be doing something."

"Suppose you find him, and he's not what you want him to be?"

"You don't understand. I need to find him. He's part of me. I may never know why Mom and Dad didn't mention him, but if I could just put flowers on his grave, acknowledge that he existed—"

Harry dried his hands and picked up a copy of the letter. "You know how much it's going to cost you to mail all these out?"

"Why are you being so negative?"

"I'm just trying to prepare you for disappointment."

"Well, don't," she warned, eyes alight. "I can do that for myself."

He succumbed to a stab of self-indulgent fear. He was losing his heart to Felicia and she was caught up in her search for her brother. What did he know about love anyway? Except the short end. He was tempting Providence to excess and couldn't seem to help it.

He moved around the counter, and put his arms around her waist and nuzzled her. "Soft neck...sweet neck..." he murmured.

"You're welcome for supper," she told him.

His head came up. "That sounds awfully like 'Good night.'"

"You'll make a fine lawyer, you're fast on the uptake."

"I'm being punished for something?"

"I have things to do. You did say you could take it or leave it—"

"I'm going to cut my tongue out."

"Don't do that. You have a wonderful gift of gab."

"Not so wonderful if I can't convince you to let me stay and do a little light necking."

"We old-fashioned women have appearances to keep up you know."

Harry gave it up. He suspected she was withdrawing into her untouchable center where no one was allowed. He was afraid to ask and lose the ground he'd gained. He held her tight for a long moment, aware of every inch of her. "I'd better hit the books."

Irrationally, Felicia felt unsettled, as if there were some strange malady attacking her soul. It was the old feeling of chaos. She was caught in a spiderweb of impulses. And she was beginning to think one of those impulses was love of Harry Pritchard. It was on the tip of her tongue to blurt it out and ask him to stay, but she was afraid. She needed time to herself. Gently she touched the small injury on his head. "I'll see you tomorrow?"

"Tomorrow," he echoed. He waited in the hall until he heard Felicia's lock click into place.

SMILING SLIGHTLY to herself and feeling wonderfully secure, Felicia leaned against the closed door. She felt as if Harry had taken a little piece of her innermost self with him.

Later, she sat by the telephone, staring at it. There was no one to call. Zelda was off in Texas, her mother off in Heaven. *I wish you were here, Mom. I miss you so much. Did you ever plan to tell me about Thomas Adam? Is that what you called him?*

Felicia picked up the letter.

No record of his death in California or bordering states.

Could he truly be alive?

She felt a spreading heat of excitement.

If Thomas Adam was alive, she'd have two important people in her life. Impulsively she hugged herself.

Thomas Adam Bennington and Harry Pritchard . . . the Third, she reminded herself, smiling.

Chapter Ten

The brightening day touched Felicia's cheeks. Telling herself she had much more to do than sit in the sun and daydream she moved from her perch on the windowsill. If she was going to live her life in a perpetual state of flux she couldn't do it without sustenance. She padded barefoot toward the kitchen. An envelope lay at the base of the door. Puzzled, she picked it up.

A note from Harry, slipped under the door. "My schedule got away from me today, but how about Friday?" was scribbled in his bold, slanting penmanship on the back of the envelope.

Inside were tickets to a charity function to be held at the renowned and renovated Roosevelt Hotel in Hollywood. Black tie. Black tie? Even with her artist's vision she couldn't imagine Harry in tux and tie.

Events in Hollywood meant movie stars and luminaries. Envelope in hand she went to her closet. That settled it. She couldn't go. She had nothing whatsoever to wear. Using a felt tip pen, she wrote "Sorry, no" in big print and taped the envelope to his door.

"I CAN'T JUST sit here watching you," Clare said. "Pass me some of those. I'll fold and stuff, you lick and stamp. I can't bear the taste of U.S. Government issue glue."

Felicia arched a brow. "Is there a difference between civilian and government glue?" The sky was blue, the garden cheerful; the sound of Alphonse's rake hummed like a metronome as he cleaned up fallen jacaranda blooms. She was wondering if she'd been too hasty in declining Harry's invitation.

"Stamp glue tastes different from envelope glue doesn't it? And even if it doesn't, I got a smile out of you. We've been worried about you, Felicia. You've seemed lackadaisical since your mother's funeral. You used to zip in and out of the building, always in a happy rush."

"Thanks for the thought, I'm fine now."

"The business with Lila has disturbed you, hasn't it?"

Felicia shrugged. "A little." *How did Harry come by that invitation, anyway?* Black-tie charity affairs cost upwards of a hundred dollars a guest.

"Now you want to find your brother's grave. Is that healthy? It's not like he was lost in war—"

"He's been lost to me. It may seem strange, but I somehow feel close to him. I have to do this."

"You know best." Clare's eyes tracked Alphonse for a while before they came back to Felicia. "Do you think Harry can keep a secret?"

"I suppose so. Why?" *It was a couples affair— dining, dancing. Harry needed a date.*

"He wants to interview me and Mildred for his thesis, but he says I've got to tell him how I hid the money. I don't want him to tell Alphonse. It's my ace in the hole. Alphonse is wearing down, I think. I'm certain he'll give in." She issued a theatrical sigh. "I hate being an eighty-year-old virgin."

Felicia swallowed a smile. "Some would say that chastity is the greatest of virtues."

"Pooh. The only people who say that are women who can't get a man and men who're looking for virgins—the nubile kind. You're not a virgin—"

"Clare."

"Well, you're not. So, tell me what to expect."

"Ask Mildred, she's had much more experience."

"Mildred won't discuss it. According to her, her entire sex life was patriotic! For God and country."

"Then watch the late show."

"I try, but I can't seem to stay awake for the good parts. Anyway, they never show the actuality. Once I even tried to get inside one of those adult book stores near Venice Beach, but this huge man blocked the way, said it wasn't the place for sweet old grandmas like me."

"Clare . . . you're hopeless."

"I'm not. But Alphonse could be. Do you think that's it? Is he too old?"

"Ask Ann Landers."

"She says not."

"You wrote and asked?"

"No, somebody else did, saved me the trouble."

"Do you love Alphonse?"

Clare cast her gaze in his direction again. "I get a tingly feeling inside sometimes." She gave Felicia a coy look. "Do you love Harry?"

Who would he ask now that she had refused to go? She began to gather up letters and put them back in a cardboard box. "Clare, thanks for your help. I just remembered, I have some shopping to do."

Twenty minutes later she was on her way. She snatched the envelope from Harry's door and replaced it with a note that said only: "You're on!" If he wanted more details he'd have to make time to find out.

"You're no longer on the force, Harry, I can't let you into the computer."

From his perch on a nearby desk, Harry wadded up his paper cup and tossed it toward the overflowing trash can. He missed. "You still make lousy coffee."

His friend and former colleague didn't smile. "When you get to be a big-shot lawyer you can hire a secretary to brew yours. Look, you want a good feed, come over to the house and see the new kid—"

"All I want is a quick peek at the Rossini data. I need it for my thesis, Women in the Criminal Justice System; Perpetrators or Victims. It's all I need to get my degree—"

Joe frowned. "Twist my arm, why don't you?"

"What's a quick look between friends, Joe? The case is ten years dead, solved. Gunny and Hansen had no problem with giving me the photographs. My professor is even getting permission for me to interview the perp at Spadra."

"Fat lot of good that'll do you. She's Loony Tunes."

"Right. That's why I need to see the data . . . for verification of the background stuff."

Joe nodded. "After eleven tonight."

"Hey, I'm here now. I've got subpoenas to deliver tonight."

"Squeeze in ten minutes."

Harry sighed and stood up. "Deal."

"One more thing," Joe said. "Why're you doing a thesis on female perps anyway?"

"My professor's got a thing for women."

Harry left the precinct and stood on the plaza in the sun. He had a thing for women, too. Or at least for one particular woman and she was driving him crazy. She operated by curious rules. One minute loving, the next, off in some world of her own—with no gate passes to any comers.

"The only time I ever talked to myself was when I was having woman trouble."

Harry snapped out of his reverie. "Manny, how you doin?" He was genuinely pleased to see the old man. Manny had been panhandling this block for more years than anyone could remember.

"I'm doin' better'n you look. You got worries?"

"You were right the first time."

"Woman trouble! I knew it." Manny shook his head. "Cops are romantics—don't face reality. You got to recognize what a woman wants, son."

"You know the answer to that one, eh?"

"It ain't nice to take that tone with your elders. An' yes, I know. A woman wants a marriage that's durable—like astroturf. That way she can walk all over you an' it don't show."

Harry laughed.

Manny shook a finger at him. "It ain't funny. It's the truth."

"I'm not laughing, Manny." He reached into his pocket. "What's the price of a cuppa these days?"

"A fiver."

Harry looked hard at the old man. Manny was grinning. He was unshaven but he had all his teeth.

"When I first came to the precinct you were asking for a quarter."

"Inflation knocked it up to a dollar. The other four are for the advice."

Harry handed over a five-dollar bill. "You're not poor, are you, Manny? How much have you got stashed away?"

Manny shuffled along, accompanying Harry to the corner. "Oh, better'n a hundred thousand, I'd guess."

Harry stopped at the curb and stared down at the man. "You're joking."

"I ain't. But I can't quit panhandling cops now, I'm an institution. You know how it is." He patted Harry on the back. "Light's green, this is as far as I go. Glad to see you up an' around again, Harry. Heard tell it was touch 'n' go with your legs. Get straight with your woman now. No tricks. A woman can't abide sneaking. You don't wanna end up like me. Money ain't the be-all."

Harry decided Manny wasn't far wrong. He drove back to the Catalina Arms. He wanted to retract his invitation to Felicia to the charity event. For him it would be work and Felicia might see that as something sneaky that he hadn't explained. He'd have to talk her out of going. Talk to her face to face.

She didn't answer his knock. He went around back and up the fire escape. Her window was closed, drapes pulled. He knocked the doors of all the other tenants. Only Lila answered, opening her door a sliver. In the background he could hear birds chirping.

"Have you seen Felicia?"

Lila jerked. "Who?"

"The tenant in apartment six."

"We don't know her."

Talking to the old woman was like talking to a bowl of cold syrup. "Sure you do. About this high, dark hair—you were in her apartment last night."

"I was only looking for my—" Lila blinked and Harry was suddenly faced with a wall of silence.

"What about Clare or Mildred?" he asked.

"What about them? A couple of silly gossips." She closed the door in his face.

"Right," he said. "Nice to see you again."

Leaving his own door open, he marked time in his apartment. He stacked dishes, exercised, took a shower. Still no Felicia. He had to pick up subpoenas before the offices closed. When he left the building he felt eyes upon him. He looked back. Lila was peeking out from behind her curtains.

Before he pulled away from the curb he glanced up at the window again. She was still there. His instincts tried to tell him something wasn't right. He chastized himself for being suspicious. Since he'd been off the force he'd tried to mainstream himself, get acclimatized to the ordinary citizen and his peculiarities.

After all, there weren't bad guys behind every bush.

FELICIA ADMIRED the dress for the umpteenth time. Elegantly black, it had rolled ribbon straps, a fitted bodice, a layered, flowing skirt with handkerchief-point hemline. She'd found it on the half-price rack of a specialty boutique. Wonder of wonders, it fit perfectly.

With great care she put it back inside the zippered bag and hung it on the back of her bedroom door.

Harry was out. She expected him any time. She listened for sounds from his apartment—the shower, windows being raised. There was only silence.

She paced. She nibbled a piece of cold, leftover chicken. She finished stuffing and stamping envelopes.

The telephone rang. She leaped to answer it. Wrong number.

She reviewed her budget and balanced her checkbook.

She sat at her drafting table and made sketch after sketch of Harry.

Delivering subpoenas was dangerous work. Maybe he was lying dead somewhere, or in a hospital emergency room.

He was tough.

He couldn't outrun a broom!

At midnight she went to bed.

She'd go over and invite him for coffee first thing in the morning.

MORNING CAME and Harry still wasn't in. Restless, Felicia mailed the letters with a silent prayer and went over to the float barns.

The barns were a beehive of activity and noise. Somewhere deep in the barn a float bed motor was being tested. Machines whirled, spitting out streams of foam, giving wire-screened figures bulk and dimension.

Harry finally discovered Felicia atop a ladder sculpting the face of a well-known comic. He admired her skill and waited until she pushed back her goggles to examine her progress. Then he called her name.

She turned off the welding flame and came down the ladder, smiling. "Hello."

"I thought I might find you here. Can I buy you lunch?"

"Where were you last night?"

"Working."

"All night?"

He pursed his lips. She sounded mad. "I sat up with a sick friend, ran into a poker game—"

Felicia stiffened. "You don't owe me an explanation."

He remembered Manny's advice. "The dull truth is I spent the night trying to deliver a subpoena."

"Did you?"

"The guy stayed one jump ahead of me all night," he admitted, looking boyishly harmless. "But don't worry, I'll catch up to him. "The goggles had left their imprint on her cheeks. He reached out with thumb and forefinger, smoothing her skin. "Lunch or not?"

They went around the corner to Rosie's, whose claim to fame was gargantuan hamburgers served with beribboned toothpicks the size of darts. The sport was to launch one's toothpicks into the ceiling.

Harry missed.

Felicia's aim was better. "More practice," she said, smiling and trying to keep a tight rein on the signals she sent to Harry. "Why'd you come looking for me, besides to invite me to lunch?"

"A couple of things. I had access to a computer with national hookup last night. I ran your brother's name through."

Felicia held her breath. "Why?"

"To see if he had a police record, traffic violations—"

"Did he?"

"Nope."

She exhaled. "He was born, we can't locate a death certificate..."

"I hate to mention it but there are a hell of a lot of John Does in limbo."

"I'll find him. I know I will. Tommy and I are connected."

"Tommy?"

"Thomas Adam Bennington is too formal."

"You expect to find him alive and well?"

"Maybe not well. And I'm still a little scared to believe he's alive." She closed her eyes. "But if he were, I'd have family." She looked at Harry. Her irises were very gray, very dark. "You said there were a couple of things...?"

"About Friday night—"

"I'm looking forward to it."

"It's just one of those Man of the Year things sponsored by some civic club or other."

"The proceeds are going to quake victims in San Francisco. I think it's wonderful that you're participating."

He kept smiling though his lips felt cramped. "I thought you might refuse, being in mourning for your mother and all—"

"My mother didn't believe in mourning beyond funerals. After Dad died, we had 'memory time.' I miss her, but I know she wouldn't want me to stop my life." Felicia was suddenly, uncharacteristically shy. "I bought a smashing dress."

Harry felt sick. Women who owned new dresses wanted to wear them, show off, have fun. "Uh, Felicia..."

Felicia looked at him. His smile was not his usual, but something decorative, utilitarian. Clarity dawned.

"You regret asking me. You have somebody else in mind."

"Not exactly. Listen, the law firm I work for gave me those tickets. I have to try to deliver a subpoena at the party. The guy we're trying to reach will be there. He generally hides behind a barrage of secretaries." Watching her face, he knew he was playing with a poor hand. "We can still go, though. You and me. We can have fun."

"And maybe get chased with a broom again? Or worse? No thanks." She was disappointed. She thought about her lovely new dress hanging in her closet. And now she had no place to wear it. Would Harry ever see her in it?

"Food, dancing, celebrities in a historic old hotel? C'mon."

"Lumpy gravy, violins, has-beens in a ghost-ridden ballroom," she countered.

He reached for Felicia's hand. "I'll be the envy of every man there. And I promise you there won't be any trouble."

She hesitated. "You're going to wear a tux?"

"Yep, with a pink cummerbund."

"Pink!" Felicia laughed. "Okay, I'll go. Pink. That I have to see."

FELICIA RUSHED HOME from the barns each day, expecting an avalanche of response to the letters.

She got bills, advertisements and a postcard from Zelda. On Friday ten of the letters were returned, addressee unknown. Felicia propped them on her dresser, puzzling over them as she got ready for her date with Harry.

Nursing homes and private-care centers went out of business. She knew that. Ten returns out of two hundred weren't enough to worry about. And at least none of those ten were from her home county. That meant one hundred ninety inquiries had probably reached their destination.

At seven o'clock Harry knocked on her door. For a moment they stared at each other, speechless.

Harry said, "My God, you're beautiful." His voice was husky.

He wore the tuxedo with elan. It emphasized his broad shoulders; his auburn hair was shower damp and curling over his collar. Felicia's heart leaped. "You look a bit out of the ordinary, yourself."

Mildred arrived with the antique beaded bag she was loaning Felicia to complement her outfit. This once her sharp tongue and wit stayed sheathed. She oohed and aahed, insisting Harry and Felicia allow Clare and Alphonse a look. The tenants followed them out to the curb and waited while Harry ushered Felicia into his car.

"You look just like a prince and princess," gushed Clare.

Felicia was mortified. "They're dears, but they're overdoing it."

Harry disagreed. "No. Tonight, magic is in the air."

At the hotel they joined elegantly clad couples streaming into the ballroom. As they passed through the lobby, Harry tugged Felicia to a mirror-backed wall. "Stare into that. What do you see?"

"Us."

"Marilyn Monroe always checked her hair and makeup in that mirror when she came into the hotel. There's a story that her reflection is often seen in it."

Felicia suddenly felt cold. "Harry—can we stay away from ghosts and crime scenes tonight?"

"Absolutely."

Their table was very near the speaker's dais and at the edge of the dance floor. Their six table mates were a mixture of lawyers, their wives and a research scientist. Harry knew only one of the men. But conversation didn't lag, especially after it was learned that Felicia designed floats.

The food was excellent, the speeches fast and witty. Harry paid extraordinary attention. Felicia was impressed. Under the table she put her hand on his thigh. He looked at her and smiled.

One of the men on the dais kept catching Felicia's eye. His wrinkled flesh hung on his face. He winked at her. She smiled politely. Harry growled. "The bastard is flirting with you."

"He's the honoree. He's probably just nervous."

He's going to be a hell of a lot more than nervous before the evening is out, Harry thought.

The tables were cleared and crumbed using tassled wisk brooms and miniature gold-plated dustpans. Champagne was served, the lights dimmed and the band started.

Harry took Felicia onto the dance floor, circled his arms about her and sighed.

"Harry, we have to move."

He stumbled through a two-step.

Understanding dawned on Felicia. "You can't dance."

"I can manage a little rhythm in my hips. Can't you feel it?"

Felicia laughed.

The Man of the Year tapped Harry on the shoulder. "Share this lovely creature, sport."

"No."

"Harry..." Felicia said sotto voce.

Unhappily he stood aside.

The man took Felicia into his arms. He smelled as if he'd bathed in after-shave and showered in cigar smoke. Felicia wrinkled her nose, but told him "Congratulations on your award."

Harry followed them around the crowded dance floor. When the man tried nuzzling Felicia's ear, Harry tapped him on the shoulder. "My turn, Jack."

The man frowned. "The name's not Jack, mister. It's Sheldon Witney."

Harry thrust out his hand. "Harry Pritchard."

Witney hesitated, then accepted Harry's outthrust hand. He looked at Felicia. "Next dance is—" He looked at the folded paper Harry had left in his palm. "What's this?"

"It's a special award," Harry said. "Sorry it's not framed. Subpoenas usually aren't."

Sheldon Witney's face went slack, then filled with outrage. He struck out at Harry with a meaty fist and missed his target. His fist landed on the temple of an unsuspecting gentleman nearby. The man fell, taking his elegantly clad dancing partner with him. The woman yelped. The man came up off the floor and plowed headfirst into Witney.

"Fight! Fight" someone yelled drunkenly.

Pandemonium erupted.

Harry turned, spotting Felicia standing at the edge of the dance floor, her expression one of horror. He waded through the milling sequin- and silk-clad crowd. Once at her side he grabbed her elbow and ushered her out the nearest exit. "Sorry about that."

"You promised me no trouble."

"Hold on."

He passed the valet his ticket with a five-dollar bill. The car was brought around. Felicia fumed. "I ought to take a cab home."

Harry thrust out his jaw. "Look, you wanna hit something, hit me. Go on."

The valet was watching and grinning.

Felicia held her anger in abeyance only until she'd slid gracefully into the car.

"I don't want to hit you. What I want is never to see you again."

"The guy had it coming. Man of the year, my eye. He's been married thirty years and has some trinket on a string. She had his baby, now he won't support the kid. People who bring babies into the world ought to take care of them."

"You're so upright and moral."

"I was just doin' my job."

Felicia refused to look at him. "We've had this conversation before."

"What're you so angry about? We were having a good time until Witney started throwing punches and made a scene. He deserved what he got. He was putting the make on you."

"I was handling it."

"I didn't like watching it."

"You don't own me."

They parted company in neutral territory—the middle of the hall.

Chapter Eleven

Lila held the medicine container tightly in her hand. "I won't throw them out, Sadie, I won't. You know I have to take them or I'll have bad dreams. The doctor said—"

Sadie snorted. "I'm in your heart. I'm your best friend. Is that how you pay me back for all these years? Haven't I been with you since you could remember? Now you want me to leave."

"No! You know that's not true."

"Take those pills and I'll disappear forever. You know that."

Lila didn't like it when Sadie was so insistent. "I don't want to go away, either, Sadie. You never tell me what you do while I'm gone. I get mixed up."

"It's just for a little while, dear. I can handle Ernest for you. You know I can. If we leave it to you, he'll catch you in a weak moment and you'll sign those papers. You know you will. And that woman has got to be punished."

"Punished?" Lila felt terror wash over her. Sadie had insisted Percy get punished and he had disappeared. Then the police had come. She shook her head, trying to sort out her memories. No, the police had come when Sadie vandalized apartment six. "I don't care about the papers," she said passionately. "I'll sign them. Maybe Ernest will let me see the children then."

Sadie sighed, a barely audible waft of air. Lila heard so many noises lately. Sometimes she couldn't even make out Sadie's voice among them.

"Why should we give up that property to Ernest? If there's a buyer, the money can be paid to you. Why, we could have new clothes, go to the theater. We could move into something other than this dump."

"But you wanted to live here, Sadie."

"Only until we get your necklace back."

"We'll never find it. We've searched everywhere."

Sadie laughed mirthlessly. "My dear, I can get her to tell me where it's hidden." She hovered like a sweet warm breath about Lila. "Come along, let's flush those nasty pills down the drain."

Lila tightened her grip. "No."

Sadie pushed her over to the bird cage. Lila trembled. "Get away from the Tweedledee, Sadie."

Sadie put her hand into the cage and coaxed a bird onto her finger. She stroked the delicate feathers, then slowly her fingers inched up to the tiny neck and began to squeeze. Lila watched in horror. "Stop! Stop! Please stop..."

"I'll take good care of your birds, Lila. I promise, I'll feed them bananas, keep the cage clean...if only you'll discard the pills."

"I don't want to," Lila choked. But she went to the kitchen and emptied the pills into the sink. Sadie turned on the hot water, allowing it to run until the capsules melted and disappeared down the drain.

"There now, that wasn't so difficult was it?"

"But where will I be, Sadie? I never know where I am when you make me go away. I get scared."

She felt Sadie gently stroking her hair. "You'll be someplace warm and safe where no one can hurt you. I'll be taking such good care of you, Lila. You're everything to me. I won't let any harm come to you."

"You'll feed my Tweetie Birds?"

"Absolutely."

Lila curled up on the sofa. "What about my necklace?" She could almost feel the opals at her throat, glowing and elegant.

"I'll get your necklace back."

"But you won't mess up her apartment again, will you? She's been nice to me, Sadie."

"I'll just ask her for it, as polite as you please."

Lila faded into sleep. Sadie watched.

THEY MADE A POINT of ignoring each other. If Harry was in the garden interviewing Clare or Mildred for his thesis, Felicia didn't carry out her garbage.

When Felicia was on the fire escape misting her plants, Harry took the long way round to the garden.

When mischance had them collecting mail at the same moment in the downstairs hall, Felicia neither spoke nor acknowledged him. She'd never felt so lonely in her life.

To make matters worse, by the end of the second week she'd had only twenty-three responses to the letter. None of them had ever had the care of Thomas Adam Bennington.

She began to fantasize about Tommy, seeing him alive. He was kin. He was her alter ego. He was family. They shared common traits, looked alike and ate the same foods. Her thoughts about having a twin went on and on, as lavish and ornately detailed as the floats she designed.

The deeper, darker mystery of why her parents had not acknowledged his existence to her, and why they had sent him away, she refused to think about.

Their birthday was only a week away. How wonderful it would be if she had found a trace of him by then.

No matter how engrossed she was with daydreams, when she went out she took special care that her apartment was secure—doors and windows locked.

When she was home, and he was home, every sound from Harry's apartment seemed to penetrate the silence. There was the tap-tap-tap of his two-fingered typing. The thumping of him exercising. She could hear him singing in the shower. She often heard his telephone ring. If he sometimes chatted with Alphonse late in the evening, when he returned from jogging, his voice carried up into her bedroom.

She missed him, and she wondered if he missed her.

She tried to tell herself she didn't need him in her life.

Yes, you do, replied a tiny inner voice.

Disgusted, Felicia ducked her head beneath her pillow. She was getting as bad as Lila about holding conversations with herself.

T*HE SUN HAD* long ago moved out over the Pacific. The moon was up but invisible through the smog. Harry's apartment was finally silent as a tomb and he was nowhere about. Using the soft shaft of light from her bedroom, Felicia went out to mist her plants. Her hearing was acute, attuned as it was to listening for Harry. From somewhere below came the muffled sound of sobbing. Felicia cocked her head and went down a few steps.

"Lila?"

"Go away."

Felicia went a few steps farther down. Mildred was sitting on the stoop, pale and disheveled in the feeble yellow glow given off by the porch light above her.

"Mildred? Is that you crying? I thought Lila—"

"Leave me alone."

"Let me sit with you."

"No." Mildred waved a damp hanky. "Go on back upstairs."

Felicia held her position on the steps. "You're upset," she said, amazed at Mildred's unusual display of tears and overflowing emotions.

Mildred sniffed and took a swipe at her nose. "Harry's writing me up as a perpetrator in his thesis. He's writing that getting married twenty-seven times is aberrant behavior brought on by misdirected patriotic fervor." She looked up at Felicia. "You know what he's writing about Clare? That's she's a victim created by male corporate structure and society's attitude toward women." She hunched over her knees and began to cry in earnest once again.

"What's going on down there?" Harry's voice came from above Felicia. "Can't a man get any sleep around here?"

Suddenly it mattered very much to Felicia that Harry should be kind to Mildred and Clare. They were, after all, more than just neighbors, they were friends, surrogate mothers. She realized how deeply attached she'd become to them. Harry had no right to be so mean.

"You insensitive clod," she yelled at him. "You've hurt Mildred's feelings."

"What?" he came down the fire escape. He was clad only in pajama bottoms.

Felicia bristled. "You heard me."

"Felicia, wait..." Mildred pleaded.

"No! Somebody needs to tell him where to get off. He has no right to just bounce into our lives and cause havoc."

"Bounce? Me? What havoc?"

Felicia tried to avoid noticing how appealing Harry looked with his hair mussed and curled over his brow. In the shadowy light his shoulders were a wide line that broke with rippling suppleness.

"You don't think, Harry. You just plow over other people's emotions."

"It's not Harry's fault," said Mildred in a small voice.

Felicia's gaze moved from Harry above her to Mildred below her. "But you said—"

"What Harry is writing is the truth. I agreed to that. It's Clare...her double chins are just quivering with moral superiority. She's trying to lord it over me. She's no better than I am! We're both ex-cons."

"You're both wonderful," consoled Felicia.

"I would have just as much money as she does, except I spent it on all those dear boys and their families. I had responsibilities!"

"I've always found you responsible," Felicia agreed, wondering how she was going to get past Harry who had settled down on the fire escape to listen. She spared him a quick glance, then leaned farther over the railing. "Come upstairs, Mildred. I'll make a pot of tea."

"Thanks, no. I feel better now. You're a sweetheart, Felicia. I'll just go tell Clare where to stick her superior attitude and her money. I've been telling her that for years. I just haven't pointed out where."

Mildred got up and went inside.

"Satisfied?" Harry said into the sudden silence.

Felicia didn't trust herself to move up the steps and into his space. "What is there to be satisfied about?"

"You've been trying to put me in my place since the moment we met. Makes you feel good all over doesn't it?"

"I mistook you for a vandal."

"What're you mistaking me for now? A fool?"

She made a tiny gesture of surrender with her hand. "Oh, Harry, stop, please. I'm miserable."

"Give a little and take it all back and then some, that's— What'd you say?"

"I'm miserable."

Harry cleared his throat. "Because of me?"

She sat down on the steps below him. "Somehow or other."

Harry was caught by the glow in her eyes and said, "Want to talk about it?"

"I can't."

"Sure you can."

Felicia knew better. If she blurted out that she loved him, wanted him, he'd accuse her of trying to trap him. "I'm just a bit blue."

"What's a little blue between friends?"

Her heart sank. Friend. So that's how he thought of her. She shrugged. "You love her don't you?"

"Who?"

"Your wife."

Damn! How was he to handle this? "No."

"You marry people when you don't love them?"

"Them? I was only married once. I thought I loved her when I married her. I was infatuated. I thought it was the greatest thing in the world. I was wrong." But he hadn't been wrong. At the time he'd loved Rita with all his heart. Looking back, he could see that Rita had just liked the excitement of falling in love. Must have. Else why the string of lovers behind his back?

"And now?"

Now? What the hell was she getting at? He wasn't about to settle his problem with her sitting out here on a rusted metal fire escape clad only in pajamas. He felt naked. "Now, I'm not married, I don't love my ex-wife, and I'm tired of just playing at being grown up."

"Life is hard," Felicia said dispiritedly.

"It sure is," he said, and didn't know if he was consoling Felicia or himself. If she so much as crooked a finger at him he knew he'd leap to wrap himself around it.

"How's your thesis coming?" she asked, sensing his reluctance and moving on to another topic.

"Getting down to the wire now. Got a couple interviews to do at Spadra and then it's a wrap."

"Spadra? Isn't that where they put the criminally insane?"

"Sure is." He gave a small laugh. "Not afraid they'll keep me, are you?"

Felicia managed a ghost of a smile. "Can you be locked up for inviting trouble?"

"I had a teacher once who said we are all in prisons of our own making."

"I'd agree with that." Talk of criminals and prison was adding to her melancholy. She changed the subject again. "You're looking forward to working for the district attorney, aren't you?"

"It'll be a regular paycheck," he said flippantly. Then, "No, it's more than that. I'm not saying every crime can be solved, or that justice prevails in every instance. But working for the DA puts you more in touch with justice, with the way the system works. Sometimes the only time the little guy gets his day in court is when he can stand up in the witness box and say, 'That's the man who hit me, or stole my television...or whatever.'" Damn! He sounded as if he was preaching from a soap box. "So, how's your letter campaign?"

Harry felt split in two: part of him on the sidelines waiting for he didn't know what, and the other part playing out some role he didn't quite understand. He gave a thought to taking Felicia into his arms and losing himself in her silken flesh. Wrong, he told himself. Better to go with the flow and not make waves. Right now he felt even closer to Felicia than when they'd made love. This was sharing.

"Not so good."

"It's early yet," he commiserated. "It may take a while. You're asking folks to check back thirty years."

Her eyes dominated her face, enhancing her mute vulnerability and her appeal. His brain was sending out signals, a warning. Too late, he thought. I'm lost.

"I keep hoping Tommy is alive, that we'll meet on our birthday. It's scary."

"If he's anything like you, he'll be—"

"What?"

"Stubborn, cheeky, impossible to live with," *or without*, he admitted silently. His mind clicked back to Thomas Adam's birth certificate. "Your birthday is June seventh, let's make that a date."

His features were craggy in the dim light, but it was his eyes Felicia was unable to ignore—his eyes on her—deep and speculative. "A date?" Suspicion highlighted the question. "How many subpoenas will we be delivering?"

Harry winced. He knew he deserved the bitterness in her voice. "None."

"What about your propensity for starting brawls?"

"I'll be the perfect gentleman, just like my mama raised me."

"You realize I'll be thirty years old, straddling that fence you put women on."

"You'll look good on the fence," he said, sensing victory. "Do we have a date?"

The weight of despair that ached inside her lifted. "All right."

He spread his knees and tapped the step. "Sit here a minute and let me put my arms around you."

"Then what?"

"Then, nothing. You look like you need a hug. What do you take me for?"

For better or worse, she thought. But she settled herself between his knees. He began to gently massage her neck and shoulders.

Her lids drooped, she tried to keep from moaning her pleasure. "That feels wonderful.... You have good hands. That was the first thing I noticed about you— your hands."

After a moment, Harry stopped, resting his hands on her shoulders. "Go on to bed before these hands get uncontrollable ideas of their own."

Urged thusly, but reluctantly, Felicia went. Before she stepped over her windowsill, she asked, "What was the first thing you noticed about me?"

"That you can distract a man from any purpose."

"Surely not you."

"Most especially me." He looked at her with eyes that were half-amused. "You talked about being scared. Suppose I'm making another mistake? Suppose I'm fooling myself into believing that you and I might make it work?" He felt a sudden stab of fear that her answer might not be to his liking. He smiled. "I'm just thinking aloud, you understand."

Felicia had the sensation she was falling off a ledge. "Of course."

She went over the windowsill into her bedroom with a lighter heart. "Good night."

He had handled that all wrong, as usual, Harry thought. After her lights winked out, he waded through the jungle of plants and sat on the sill. "Felicia?"

He heard her slight intake of breath, the rustle of sheets as she sat up. "What?"

"I wish we could look into the future."

"So do I."

"I've never been in a situation like this," he said awkwardly, protected by the dark. "I feel helpless."

"What's going to happen?"

"I don't know."

He was quiet for a moment, then she heard him chuckle.

"My dad told me once that a man may fall in love below the belt, but stays in love above the neck."

Felicia smiled into the dark. "I think I would've liked your dad."

"He was a special guy."

"You're a lot like him, I'll bet."

Harry went so still and quiet had Felicia not been looking at his silhouette she would've sworn he'd gone.

He came out of his reverie slowly. "Dad was a man who knew what he wanted and went after it."

"You have that same kind of purpose and drive."

"You think so?" he said, pleased.

"I'm positive," she answered with feeling.

"Do I detect a reservation in your tone?"

"I think you're so purposeful sometimes that you knock others aside without thinking."

"Ah. Maybe I should head off to bed while I'm still ahead."

"Pleasant dreams."

"Lately I seem to dream of you."

Felicia tried not to doubt that. "You tell incredible lies."

Harry sighed. Only to myself, he thought and stood up, flexing his knees. For a change they didn't creak or groan.

FELICIA EMERGED into the foyer and stopped. Lila was facing off with Ernest and another man who, to Felicia, had "official" written all over him. Clare, Mildred and Alphonse were hovering across the hall in the open doorway of Cora's apartment. Felicia slipped up to Clare. "What's going on?" she whispered.

"Just listen," Clare whispered back.

"You can take me to any doctor you please," Lila was saying passionately. "I'm as sound of mind as you are. I'd be delighted to have it proved."

Lila's elderly audience cheered. Ernest and his companion turned in unison and glared at the group. "Nosy busybodies," Ernest accused. He caught Felicia's eye. "Have you aligned yourself with these people?"

Felicia gave him her best smile. "These are my friends."

"And mine," said Lila, poking her son in the chest. "You get this man out of here, Ernest, and don't come back. I don't need some hotshot lawyer to tell me what's best for me. It somehow always makes my purse lighter and yours richer. Mama and Papa left that land to me—not you."

"Now, Mrs. Ross—"

Lila shoved the lawyer. "Out! You're an evil man, trying to take away what's rightfully mine."

Another cheer went up. Clare clapped her hands. "Way to go, Lila!" She elbowed Felicia. "See? I told you if she knew we supported her, she'd stand up to Ernest."

"Mother, be reasonable. You want to see the children, don't you?"

Lila sniffed. "It's too late to dangle the carrot. I have my friends now." She looked past Ernest and smiled at Mildred.

Ernest and the lawyer stepped aside and conferred in whispers. The lawyer left. Ernest looked first at the group cheering Lila and then at his mother. "You're not yourself, Mother. These people may not know it, but I do."

"I'm more myself than ever," said Lila, laughing up at him. He pivoted on his heel and stormed out of the foyer.

Alphonse offered Lila his arm. "Well done, my dear. Shall I escort you to the garden?"

Lila tittered. "Why, Alphonse."

Clare frowned. "Just a minute, you two—"

Mildred grabbed her arm. "Hold it, you're supposed to help me get Cora's apartment ready."

Clare looked at Alphonse's retreating back, watching the way Lila was leaning on his arm. "But—"

Felicia followed the older woman's gaze. Lila had a new hairstyle and the skirt she wore had an elegance of movement that caught the eye. She put an arm lightly around Clare. "Clare, I believe you're jealous."

"I am not. But you'd think Lila would have more sense of . . . of sisterhood after all we've done for her. Alphonse is—"

"Being kind," finished Mildred. "But run along if you insist. You aren't worth two hoots with a dust cloth anyway."

Clare went.

Mildred rolled her eyes. "Pitiful, isn't it?" she said to Felicia. "Eighty years old and she has her head you-know-where."

"You're feeling better yourself," Felicia prompted, smiling as she opened her mail slot.

"The other night was just a fluke," Mildred said archly. "My biorhythm was out of whack or something."

Felicia quickly scanned envelopes.

"Anything?"

Felicia shook her head.

"Well, maybe tomorrow."

"I had so hoped—" Felicia stopped. If she mentioned it was her birthday, the old folks would get into a dither, plan an impromptu party and there would go her evening with Harry.

"Cora's coming home on the twenty-ninth... sooner, if she can master the walker," Mildred was saying. "They took her body cast off today."

"Terrific," Felicia said, projecting an enthusiasm she couldn't quite feel.

Mildred touched her arm. "You don't want to waste your life looking for your brother, Felicia."

"I'm not. It just would be nice to have family."

"You have family," Mildred said sternly. "You have me and Clare and Alphonse and Cora. Even Lila has possibilities now."

Felicia smiled. "I know, and I love you all."

"Good. Now scoot. Go upstairs and check on Harry. He's layered in ice bags."

"He's hurt himself, again?"

"He dropped some exercise equipment. I thought we were having another quake what with the noise he made crashing to the floor."

Felicia took the stairs two at a time.

Chapter Twelve

Harry was sitting on a straight-backed chair, his right foot plunged into water with ice cubes floating in it. Felicia recognized Mildred's yellow mop bucket, the one she stored near the back stoop.

Harry greeted her with a smile that was disarming, sexy and somewhat apprehensive. "Before you say a word, I know what you're thinking—"

The adrenaline rush that had carried her upstairs subsided only to be replaced by unexplainable annoyance. "Oh, now you read minds?" she asked in a sepulchral voice.

"You're thinking I did this on purpose as an excuse to cancel our date."

What she'd been thinking was that he was hurt and suffering and needed her. But of course he didn't. He was perfectly capable of taking care of himself. By some mercurial human quirk, that exacerbated her annoyance. "What I think is that you're the clumsiest man I've ever known. How could you drop something on your foot?"

He rolled with her attack. "Easy," he said affably. "I was trying to press a couple hundred pounds. The phone rang and the bar slipped out of my hands."

"You could've maimed yourself!"

"I did." He lifted his foot from the bucket and dried it. "I suppose I'll have to wear sandals for a few days." He frowned. "People will think I'm a hippie reject."

Looking at his swollen toes made Felicia queasy. She took a deep breath. "Probably you should bandage that."

Her tiny offering of comfort was what he'd been listening for. He limped over to her. "All is not lost. Your birthday celebration is still on."

"Do you realize that every time you ask me out to eat—we don't."

"I've ordered wine, pizza—" He took her into his arms.

She wriggled free.

He didn't know whether to feel guilty or angry. He dropped his arms. "Damn it, Felicia! What do you want? I didn't plan to muck up your birthday." He hobbled across the room, bent down beyond the sofa, retrieved a package and carried it back to where she stood on the threshold. "Happy Birthday," he growled, thrusting the package into her hands.

Without waiting for a response, he sat down and plunged his foot into the bucket once again. When Felicia didn't speak he said, "You're welcome."

His sarcasm went past her. She was staring at the gift. He had wrapped it himself, she could tell. The wrappings did not quite meet in the middle so that the contents were obvious—a thick, ring-bound and expensive sketch book—the kind she always lingered over but never bought herself. She felt guilt and regret at her rudeness. He'd been thoughtful, kind and gallant. Her chest tightened, her eyes began to burn.

Wordlessly she picked up a pencil from the card table, sat down on his sofa and opened the sketch book and began to draw.

Harry watched her out of the corner of his eye and remained silent.

After ten minutes she passed him the book. There were more than a dozen cartoons on the page—caricatures of a couple attempting to make love. There was dialogue beneath each: "Ouch! That's my elbow, stupid!" The one he liked best had the sheet in a lumpy ball, rotating, arms and legs poking out everywhere. The caption read "Time out!" He bit back his laughter.

In the bottom right-hand corner, in exceedingly tiny print was the underlined notation "Take Liberties." Heart beating faster, he looked at her.

Her expression was uncertain.

"Happy thirtieth birthday," he said softly.

As HE WAS UNDRESSING HER it occurred to Harry that he'd crossed some mysterious boundary. He wasn't sure of the significance, but a tremor started very low in his gut and moved rapidly upward so that it touched his very soul.

Reverently he cupped her breasts with his hands. She responded with a small sound of pleasure. It was a sound he wanted washing over him on his way into the hereafter.

He drew air into his lungs, as though it were the very last breath available for survival, and whispered her name.

With an evanescent sixth sense Felicia realized he'd crossed some critical hurdle, that he was willing to share with her his very essence. She felt both powerful and filled with need; and offered to him every little part of herself that she had held so secret.

THE PIZZA WAS DELIVERED hot and crispy, the wine, chilled. Harry urged her out of his bed. "C'mon. It's your birthday supper. Let's eat while it's hot."

She stretched languidly. "Okay. Toss me your robe."

Harry decided to try a more direct tack. "Don't you want to put on your clothes?"

She glanced at his bedside clock and grinned impishly. "I'll just have to take them off again—won't I? Let's eat in bed."

"Too much distraction. Put on your clothes."

"I like you distracted."

Harry pursed his lips. There was obviously nothing he could do to change her mind. "Okay, but don't say I didn't warn you."

He went back into the kitchen, mumbling as he rummaged in cabinets for wineglasses. He finally gave up the hunt, washed and set out a pair of coffee mugs.

"I have a couple of glasses," Felicia offered, tightening the sash of his robe about her waist. Knee-length on Harry, it reached almost to her ankles.

She was decently covered but the robe told all, Harry knew, and that was the trouble. Big trouble. "Sure you don't want to put on a pair of jeans?"

"I'm positive." She didn't want to give up the robe, it was filled with Harry's scent. "I'll be back with those glasses in a jiffy."

As soon as she was across the hall Harry made a beeline for the stairs. He'd have to stall the old folks, say Felicia had a headache or something. He should never have borrowed that tape from Mildred or allowed her to worm out of him what he needed it for. The old ladies had insisted on baking Felicia a cake for tonight. Alphonse was to provide ice cream, Lila the candles.

Damn! He should not have succumbed to his need of her, he should've been strong. But no, he had been afraid to spoil things by refusing her.

He met the foursome on the stair landing. The ladies were front and center, Alphonse, carrying the cake on a platter, brought up the rear.

"I know," Mildred said, "we're running a few minutes late. You didn't tell her did you?"

Harry spread his arms blocking their passage. "No."

"How's your foot?" Clare wanted to know.

"Good as new. Look, there's been a change of plans."

"Harry?" Felicia peered over the bannister and froze. It took her a full ten seconds to read the situation and have it register.

Clare noticed Felicia's dishabille and giggled. "Well, now we know what Harry meant by a change of plans."

"Be quiet for once in your life," chastized Mildred. "Can't you see the poor girl is mortified? Happy birthday, Felicia."

Harry spoke up. "It was supposed to be a surprise."

Felicia was so furious she could barely speak. "You *knew*?"

"I can't win," Harry said gloomily. "I tried to get you to put your clothes on—remember?"

"Do I have to stand here all evening with this cake or what?" asked Alphonse.

Lila began to sing "Happy Birthday," the others joined in. Harry edged up the stairs singing as loud and as off-key as he sang in the shower.

Felicia couldn't make herself blame the old folks for catching her out. She suffered through it. When the tune finished, she smiled wanly.

"Sounds like I'm in the right place," came a voice floating up the stairwell.

Harry started. "Mother! What're you doing here?"

Mother? Felicia tried to make her feet move.

"Why, Harry, is this where you live? I thought the address was familiar."

Harry's arm slipped about Felicia's waist in a death grip as he began introductions. "Mom, this is Felicia—"

"Bennington?" Thea asked. "Just the person I came to see."

"Let's get off these steps," complained Mildred. "I'm getting a crick in my neck."

The group trouped upstairs. Harry disengaged his arm from Felicia's waist, and she escaped. Once in her apartment she flung herself onto her bed and contemplated Harry's iniquities while she pounded on the pillow with both fists.

Harry gave her five minutes, then went to fetch her.

"It's your birthday party, you have to put in an appearance."

"I don't have to do anything!" she said, yanking on a pair of jeans. "How could you do this to me? Why is your mother here? How does she know my name?"

"She's an astrologer, apparently your friend Zelda is one of her clients."

Felicia groaned.

"She's done your chart."

"You told me she owned a furniture store!"

"She does. This astrology stuff is a hobby."

Felicia recognized that as less than the full truth. "Not according to Zelda." She pushed him out the door. "See that balustrade. Go jump off it."

"I'll consider it after you've had cake and ice cream. The old folks are waiting. They've been planning this all afternoon. You want to hurt their feelings? They even got Lila involved. She's bustling around in my kitchen like she owns it."

Felicia *was* curious about Harry's mother. "I don't know how good a face I can put on it. You should've told me!"

"Then it wouldn't have been a surprise."

"I could've pretended to be surprised."

"That would not have been honest. I thought honesty was important to you."

"It is."

"Suppose I told you I think you're outstandingly intelligent, talented and beautiful."

Felicia glared at him.

"Suppose I told you I'm sorry I got us both into this fix?"

She looked at a spot on the floor.

"All right. I'm going in there and tell them I batted zero—"

Her head came up. "No. I'll face them, but I feel as if I'm condemned to the gallows."

"We have to sing 'Happy Birthday' again," Mildred said upon their entrance. "Felicia, dear, blow out the candles."

Hiding her dismay and carefully avoiding looking at Harry's mother, Felicia obliged. Everyone clapped.

Amid small talk she cut and served the cake while Lila scooped up ice cream.

"Finish what you were saying about my planets rising, Thea," Clare implored indicating that the outgoing and lively astrologer had won their approval and been taken into the fold.

Harry perched on a kitchen stool, ate cold pizza and behaved like Stoneface, Mt. Rushmore. Didn't he and his mother get along? Felicia wondered.

"What I want to know," continued Clare, "is if the man I'm going to lose my virginity to is in this room."

Face going pink, Alphonse quickly stood up, his starched shirt crackling. "There's a news program I'm longing to see. Good year and cheer, Felicia. Bye all."

"Now, is he *out* of the room?" Clare asked.

Thea didn't miss a beat. "Why don't you call me later," she offered, passing Clare her card. From the counter Harry rolled his eyes and made noises of irreverence. Thea caught Felicia's attention. "Harry has one great failing, he only sees me one way—Mother."

"I don't believe in all that star gazing."

"Your loss, dear heart. There's order in the universe—" she gazed about the apartment "—from which you could certainly learn something."

"How do people perceive me," asked Mildred.

"Caring, warm-hearted and orderly," Thea said.

Clare violently disagreed. "She's bossy!"

Felicia felt an odd prickling at the back of her neck as if someone or something unknown had invaded her space. She glanced over her shoulder. Lila stood behind her, her expression stark, eyes remote. "Lila?" she said softly.

Lila twitched, then spun away, hiding her face.

Mildred called Lila back. "Don't go shy on us," she said solicitously. "Come and listen to what Thea is saying about us."

"I don't want no chart done or anybody reading my mind!" Lila exclaimed and bolted from the apartment.

"Now what got her in a huff?" Clare puzzled.

Thea stood up. "Well, I must be going. Felicia, may I speak with you a moment—alone?"

It was a polite direct request. Felicia couldn't refuse. They went into the hall. "You have a lost twin . . ." Thea began.

"Harry told you."

"He asked me something about it, but he didn't mention your name. It's in your chart." She removed a thick envelope from her large purse. "Happy birthday from Zelda."

"I—thank you." She met Thea's gaze. "I feel so awkward."

"You're not interested in astrology."

"Not really—no. Well, I confess. I do read my horoscope sometimes."

"Don't be embarrassed. Harry won't admit its benefits either, but it paid the bills when he was growing up. The furniture store took a while to catch on, and by the time it did I had a host of clients and a following I didn't want to give up." She tilted her head, eyes alight. "I'll be seeing more of you, I'm sure." At the look on Felicia's face, she laughed. "I noticed the way Harry was watching you. We're going to be great friends, I can tell."

"We might be, I'm not so certain about Harry and myself."

"With Harry, life is always in flux. He's a lot like his father was—a lot of swagger and bluster. And he's afraid good things won't last." Her dark eyes were suddenly filled with a sparkling warmth. "Had I known you were involved with Harry in any way, I would've refused to do your chart at Zelda's request."

Felicia protested. "I'm not—"

Thea gently pressed her fingers to Felicia's lips, silencing her. "Read what the stars have to say. There are some interesting events coming up in your life soon." She walked over to Felicia's door and stood there for a moment. "I don't want to alarm you, but you're being approached by an extremely negative energy, it could be dangerous for you." She smiled, and in her smile Felicia could see Harry's. "You'll take care, won't you? I'll just say goodbye to Harry. The klutz. I could've told him he was accident prone today."

"Mrs. Pritchard . . . wait a minute."

"Let's not stand on ceremony. Call me, Thea."

Felicia hesitated. "All right. Thea. Will I find my brother?"

"You'll receive some word."

"But will he be dead or alive?"

"I don't know. I'm sorry. I'll ask Harry to bring you to dinner one night. Would you come?"

"I might."

"We'll leave it at that, then."

Two minutes later Clare and Mildred were walking Thea out.

Harry faced off with Felicia.

"Go on, say it," he accused. "It was a disaster."

Felicia felt unsettled, yet the few minutes spent with Thea had blunted her distress. There was something wonderfully calming about Harry's mother. Too bad it had not rubbed off on Harry. "It wasn't a disaster. Your brain may work on the wrong track sometimes, but your heart is in the right place."

"You're not mad?"

"I'm furious. But I expect I'll get over it. Meanwhile, I'll just get my clothes from your room."

"Don't run off. The evening isn't over."

"I want to be alone."

Her eyes filled with something Harry couldn't put a name to. It seemed as if whatever it was that had held her together had dissolved. He felt a twinge of guilt. He'd been thinking only of himself. A gnawing little voice inside him said she needed time to sort things out and he needed to give her the time she needed.

He put his hands on her shoulders and kissed her lightly on her forehead. "Okay, you won't get any argument from me tonight. Happy birthday," he added softly.

After she disappeared into her apartment, Harry limped into his bedroom and stretched out on his bed with his injured foot elevated. It had begun to throb. He took up the pillow with Felicia's scent upon it and hugged it to him.

He felt the certainty in his chest growing as if to squeeze the life out of him. His heart was pounding, he was tense, his fists were clenched, his muscles knotted. It was true love. Had to be.

He couldn't get out of it. On the other hand, this time he damned sure wasn't going to let it show until he was sure it was the right thing for him—and for Felicia.

"You weren't asleep, were you?"

"Zelda," Felicia said with groggy exasperation. "It's one in the morning. What would you expect me to be?"

"Partying! Celebrating. I just called to say happy birthday."

"Consider it done. Thank you—"

"Don't hang up! Did you get your chart?"

"Yes."

"You met Thea? Isn't she neat?"

"Thea is Harry Pritchard's mother. I suppose you had no idea."

"Oh, that's—what! Of course I didn't know! How could I? Oh, but Felicia! That's wonderful. I can't wait to get home and watch everything unfold. Speaking of which—would you mind checking on a couple of things at the float barns for me?"

One of Zelda's designs was eighty-five feet long and another shot thirty feet into the air. And without Zelda's notes and schematics it would be impossible to do anything with either of them. "I can't, Zelda, you know that. You have to come back."

"It's Harry isn't it?"

"Have I mentioned Harry?"

"What does your chart say about him?"

"Nothing." But it had. It had said that she could expect a transformation of her love life, a radical change. It had also said opposite from Saturn, whatever that was, meant that the relationship would be a time of testing, challenges and overcoming obstacles. Harry was most certainly all of that! She picked out something else to tell Zelda. "It says that Mercury is in retrograde," she replied dryly, recalling the quote but not its definition.

Zelda gasped. "That means a day of reckoning for you! I'll be home as soon as I can."

Felicia listened to Zelda wax on warningly about planets rising, passing, opposing the Sun and being in numbered houses ruled by conjuncts and ascendants. When she started on love-sex signs, Felicia called a halt.

She rang off and went back to bed only to discover she was wide awake. She made herself a cup of hot cocoa and settled in to reread the thick pages of her horoscope. Not that she really believed a word of it.

She searched for the part that talked about Gemini twins.

The pattern of your life may seem unique and individual with a good smattering of the unexpected popping up. One of the unexpected elements may be your twin self. At times this can seem confusing. Uncertainty and change may color your life and you thrive in a stimulating environment. Find your twin self and you will have that essential sense of unity. Concentrate your efforts!

Felicia inhaled. It was scary, how close to the truth the chart hit. She could see how astrology held such appeal for people like Zelda who scattered their energies and were reluctant to make decisions on their own.

But she wasn't like that, she thought, taking inventory.

She was levelheaded, goal oriented and practical.

She had a twin she couldn't find, yet it was as if she were seeking her own self.

She approached the boundary of loving Harry and pulled back each time, frightened of that spiritual intimacy, that oneness.

Everyone she had ever loved had been snatched from her. A coldly efficient universal law. Everyone dies.

The lingering taste of chocolate stimulated memories, replaying a montage of times she and her mother had talked the night away. What would you say to all of this, Mom?

No answer came.

SADIE SAT in the garden and stared up at apartment six. Smog was low and thick, clouding the top of the building. Frustration pulsed within her like something alive. She had not been able to corner Felicia alone or get into the apartment.

And for days now she'd had to tolerate those two old flits gabbing. She cackled softly. If only they knew.

She should've been an actress. Had wanted to be an actress, had begged Mama and Papa to let her go on stage. But, no. Lila had insisted on marriage to Percy and that was the end of Sadie's dream. Well, she was acting now and doing a good job of it. Even Ernest was fooled, like the doctors had been fooled.

She shifted her attention from her reverie to the window again. The slut! Everyone knew what she was doing with Harry. She had lured him just like she'd lured Percy, made him do evil things. Revulsion swept over Sadie.

She'd think about the knife. That always made her feel better. It was lovely and shiny. She'd been sharpening it all week. No one had noticed she'd filched it the day of the birthday party. They had not noticed at all when she'd sailed out, head high, stage exit. Lila would be so proud of her!

Sadie giggled. There was another thing Lila would be interested to know. She'd figured out how to open all the mail boxes. All it took was a nail file. Of course she had not disturbed any but the one for apartment six. She had hidden it well. She thought of envelopes stacked so neatly in her hiding place as if hugging some wonderful secret.

When the time was right, they were going to be her entrée into apartment six.

"Lila!" Mildred called. "What're you doing sitting out there? Have you forgotten? We're off to Von's to get food for Cora's homecoming. Alphonse has the car around front."

"Coming," she answered affably.

Oh, I'm good, Sadie thought, smoothing out her skirt. Even sharp-eyed Mildred with her dour unfashionable clothes and ideas doesn't suspect.

After she punished Felicia, she would thumb her nose at Mildred and Clare's pseudo elegance. She'd get all her money back from Ernest and rent a really spiffy place. She'd have them all over for dinner. Why, she might even let Lila put in an appearance.

No, better not. The birds were dead. Lila would whine, get sloppy with disgusting tears.

She was well rid of Lila.

Chapter Thirteen

"I thought I heard you out here," Harry said as he stepped over the sill and joined Felicia on the fire escape.

She smiled, but wanly. "I didn't know you were home." He was still favoring his injured foot slightly, but she noticed more than that. He was turned out with unusual smartness: slacks pressed, shirt spotless, hair combed.

He sat down beside her. Their arms touched. The nearness, the touching awakened all of Harry's senses. "You've been avoiding me all week."

She averted her eyes, looking instead into the garden where all was ready for Cora's homecoming. The little yard was pristine: a card table had been added, and both tables were draped in Clare's finest pink linen and laden with cutlery and candles. "I haven't," she lied. "I've been working late, trapped at the barns with one problem after another."

"Don't be kind on my account. If it's over, it's over."

Her stomach lurched. "I told you—there's something quirky inside me that won't—"

"Here we go again." He rolled his eyes.

"Don't pick on me."

"I'm not picking on you. We have something going for us—admit it. I admit it." There! It was said.

"I've got to find out about my brother. I can't consider myself until—"

Harry muttered an epithet. "Look, you got along for thirty years without him—who the hell needs a ghost? You've got to come to terms with this fantasy, accept reality."

"I don't need a lecture. Your mother said I'd get some word, but I haven't had so much as an advertisement in my mailbox all week. I reread my chart. It said the twenty-ninth of June would be a day of change, of reckoning, an ending and a beginning. Here it is the twenty-ninth of June and so far nothing out of the ordinary has transpired."

"Games. That's all astrology is, a bunch of weirdos clamoring for somebody to tell them how they should live."

"How can you talk about your mother that way?"

"I adore my mother. I admire her. She's tapped into a gold mine, that's all."

"It scares you."

"Nothing scares me."

"You're so tough."

"I'm sensible, down to earth." And what he wanted most on earth was elbow to elbow with him on a rusted fire escape behaving as if her world was coming to an end. "Look, you can't spend your life looking for a grave or a man who might not exist. You've got to get things in perspective."

"That's easy for you to say. It's not your twin." She cupped her knee with her hands. "You're not the one plagued with unanswered questions."

"I have a few questions I'd like answers to," he said, baiting her. One of which was, *Will you marry me?*

She left the hook dangling.

No use, Harry thought. "Well, I reckon," he mocked, "I'll mosey along. Got my interview at Spadra this evening. I want to get on the road before the five-o'clock traffic makes the drive a nightmare."

"Harry—"

"Forget it. It takes two to tango and I can see I'm dancing all by myself. And you know something? I don't like it."

"You know I'm grateful to you for all of your help."

"Grateful!" He laughed mirthlessly. "Boy, do you have a blind spot."

He moved away from her and returned to his apartment. A moment later Felicia heard his door close.

She felt utterly alone and desolate. Harry was on target, she knew. She was full of herself—selfishly so. She knew enough psychology to know she was searching for that lost child within—searching for Tommy was just an added excuse.

She was afraid she'd learn her parents had abandoned him and that would forever spoil her memories of them. She closed her eyes. Maybe she was coming to terms with her own mortality. Birthdays had a way of making that happen.

This self-exploration begged the question. What was there going to be in her life between now and death?

Harry—that's what, she decided.

His lumps, misguided ideas and his silly, macho defense mechanisms just made life with him more interesting. He had ideals and a zest for life. Working day and night didn't seem to bother him, and he was generous with his time. He gave it to her, to Clare, to Mildred and Alphonse. His personality took a little getting used to, but really, his outbursts would be easier to live with than a man who went off and sulked all day. As for matters of the heart . . . well, nobody was perfect, but in that particular area, Harry came very close.

When he returned from Spadra, she'd tell him. Make him listen. If he didn't want her—well, she'd learn to live with that or find a way to drive him out of his mind, until he gave up—or in.

Her desolation lifted.

But throughout Cora's party she was distracted. She kept glancing up at Harry's windows, waiting for the lights to switch on.

"Well, when is that gorgeous creature I've been hearing so much about going to put in an appearance?" boomed Cora during a lull in the gaiety. She was a buxom, handsome woman in her sixties. Had it not been for the walker that was parked discreetly behind her chair, one would never suspect she suffered greatly from osteoarthritis or was recovering from a broken hip. Everyone looked to Felicia for a response.

"He had to go to Spadra on an interview for this thesis. I'm sure he'll be back soon."

Sadie's hand trembled. "Spadra . . . ?" Her face took on the blank, listening look of someone considering a new and unpleasant idea.

"That's the hospital for the criminally insane," Clare informed her. "The judge sent Mildred there for an evaluation before she was sentenced, didn't he

Mildred? They thought any woman who'd take up with twenty-seven men had to be crazy as a loon. If you ask me, they should've kept her!'' she added, kindling an argument that lasted a full five minutes.

Felicia exchanged a tolerant glance with Alphonse. Cora clapped her hands with glee. She turned to Sadie. ''Aren't Clare and Mildred entertaining? Never a dull moment with those two around.''

Sadie nodded because she couldn't speak. Her head was whirling. Spadra. They knew about Spadra. She had a bad feeling. Lila was trying to get out, she could hear her crying faintly, begging. She had to stop listening. She glanced about her wildly, discovering Felicia was speaking to her. The sound of Felicia's voice drowned out Lila's.

''I haven't heard your birds chirping lately,'' Felicia said pleasantly.

You can't fool me, Sadie thought. You know they're dead. And I'm going to cut you up and be rid of you just like them. Sadie laughed. ''They're the sweetest things.''

''All recovered from the earthquake excitement?''

''Oh, yes, quite.'' She dispensed her best theatrical smile.

It was amazing, Felicia thought, how much Lila had changed over the past week or so. Gone was her curious habit of repeating herself over and over, and the vacant, frightened look she used to wear. All Lila had needed was a support group to help her break Ernest's hold on her. She returned the older woman's smile. ''Your whole face changes when you smile, Lila. You're pretty.''

''Papa always thought so,'' Sadie said, looking as innocent as any saint.

The comment struck Felicia as fey. But she could see Lila was pleased with the compliment. The poor dear, she thought with empathy. Lila probably had not been in the path of kindness often in her life. "I think I'd better see if Mildred has more coffee perked. Clare has this pot laced with Irish whiskey."

Sadie jumped to her feet. "I'll come with you."

"HOLD IT," Harry said angrily. "I didn't drive all the way out here just to be told 'Forget it.'"

The assistant to the director of Spadra sat behind the desk, steepling his fingers. "We don't give out information or discuss our patients," he said unctuously.

"We're talking about a criminal—a ward of the state. We're talking about a murderer who cut up, deboned and stacked her fileted husband on the kitchen sink. And I have permission from the judge who sent her here to interview her."

The man fidgeted. "Well, you can't."

Harry took a step forward. "Get your boss in here."

"That won't do you any good. The Rossini woman is not here."

Harry stopped in his tracks. "What the hell does that mean? She died?"

"She was released." The assistant leaned back in his chair enjoying Harry's reaction.

"You put that murderer back on the street?" To add to his disappointment over the injustice of such a release, Harry saw his thesis going down the tube.

"We have the discretion to release patients who are no longer considered dangerous. Her son accepted custody. Lila is hardly what you'd call 'on the street.'"

"Lila?" Harry breathed a silent sigh of relief. "We're not talking the same person. I want to see Lillian Rossini. I was told after dinner is—"

"She was called Lila here and, on occasion, Sadie. A true dual personality, actually."

Harry decided to take advantage of the man's knowledge to see if he could salvage something for his thesis. "Dual personality?" he repeated pleasantly, then settled his bulk into the pullman chair in front of the desk. "Sounds fascinating. Maybe you could tell me something about that. Could I quote you in my thesis? And perhaps in an article I'm planning?" He whipped out his notepad. "Maybe you'd better spell your last name for me."

"That's G-r-e-z-l-i-c-h. Ph.D. Where would you be placing the article?"

Harry gave his best smile. "I'm negotiating with two nationally known magazines. Suppose I let you know which of them I go with later."

"Of course. I'd like a copy for my files, just as a courtesy."

Harry made a squiggle on his notepad. "Done. Suppose we discuss Lillian Rossini? If she's been released, I suppose I'll have to change her name in the article—to protect her family. One never likes to injure the innocent."

"Well, under the circumstances..." agreed the assistant, beaming. "Only don't change it to 'Ross,' because the son already has—"

Harry jerked. "Ross? As in *Ernest* Ross? The real estate magnate?"

"That's the one. He sold out the butcher shops after his mother was incarcerated. He petitioned the court to have his mother's name changed too. The stigma—"

"He didn't by any chance change it to Lila Ross?"

Grezlich's eyebrows lifted. "You've done your homework, my man. The director released Lila into Ross's custody. Personally I was against it. We did a follow up, of course. But Ross had placed her in a nursing home."

Harry felt a dizzy, spinning feeling in his stomach. "Suppose he didn't keep her there. What if she were released? Is she dangerous?"

Grezlich shook his head. "Lila has always been harmless, she's the weak personality of the two. Sadie is the dangerous one. Sadie did the number on the husband, Percy, you know." He launched happily into a discourse on dual personalities. Harry only half listened. "Sadie thought she was well hidden during the time she was here. However, whenever Lila showed any aggression or balked, we knew Sadie was present."

Things were clicking in Harry's mind.

"You should've seen Lila telling Ernest off today. We're so proud of her."

"Ernest is the one who's been breaking into my apartment and trying to make it seem as if it's Lila. He wants to put her away."

Harry's scalp crawled. It had not been Ernest, but it had not been Lila either. "The Sadie personality," he said. "What is she like?"

"Vicious. Just vicious. Prim. Sex was dirty but blood wasn't. Lila couldn't stomach working in her parent's butcher shops. Sadie did the bloody work for her. Let me tell you, Sadie is very, very good with a knife. She attacked her attendants here once. We had to put her in isolation. Poor Lila was bewildered by that. Sadie always hid out at the first sign of trouble.''

Harry recalled the chicken on Felicia's counter, neatly and skilfully dismembered.

''It was Sadie who had followed Percy to the Catalina Arms and watched Percy with his mistress through a window.''

''Catalina Arms?'' Harry felt a dread in the pit of his stomach. ''There was nothing about that in the police files.''

''That's because the police arrested Lila at home, where the murder took place. She didn't know about the affair. Sadie hadn't told her. And we wouldn't have known either—except we eavesdropped on their conversations. Sadie was always scheming to get back there, and punish the mistress.''

Harry's mouth went dry. ''Punish?''

Grezlich sliced the air with his hand. ''That's what she did to Percy. She punished him for hurting Lila.''

Goosebumps erupted over Harry's entire body. ''Did Ernest Ross know of Lila's . . . Sadie's fixation with the Catalina Arms?''

''I doubt it. And anyway, what would be the use of telling him? The affair and the murder happened more than ten years ago. The woman probably isn't there any longer. To tell you the truth, Ross doesn't believe in dual personalities. I've met him. He was never really convinced that his mother killed his dad. And, she didn't. Sadie did.''

Harry's strident breathing sounded loud in his ears. ''Did Lila or Sadie ever mention which apartment the mistress lived in?''

"Oh sure. Apartment six. And Sadie convinced Lila that Percy gave the mistress Lila's opal necklace. I'll tell you, we see a lot of crazies here—" he snickered "—don't quote me on that—but the Rossini women— it's eerie, the way they'd whisper back and forth. Each of them thinks the other is real. Though we could never coax Sadie out to talk to the therapists."

"Suppose Sadie had access to the Catalina Arms today?"

The man barked a laugh. "If I lived in apartment six, I'd be watching my back."

"May I use your phone?"

Grezlich pushed it forward on the desk. "Just dial nine for an outside line."

Harry dialled Felicia's number. It rang and rang. Damn! She must still be downstairs at the party for Cora. He cradled the phone. "Sorry, but I've got to leave."

Grezlich thrust his card into Harry's hand. "If you have any more questions."

"Just one. Why the hell was Lila turned loose?"

"Actually, as long as she's medicated—"

"But if she isn't?"

Grezlich smiled wryly. "Say hello to Sadie."

Harry bolted for his car.

THE PARTY WAS OVER. Clare was giggling and tipsy. Mildred fussed. "You're ready for bed, old girl."

"Who're you calling an old girl?"

"The only one among us who is drunk, that's who."

"Priggish old hen. What's a few nips?"

"The difference between sober and not." Mildred heaved her companion out of the chair and hitched an arm around her. "Alphonse, you'll help Cora inside?"

"I am a bit weary," said Cora. "Still on hospital hours, I think. But thank you all. It's been a lovely homecoming." She beamed at Felicia. "I suppose I'll meet Harry tomorrow, but it's his mother who sounds interesting. I think I'll have her do my astro chart."

Sadie began to clear the tables.

"I'll help you with that," Felicia said.

"No. It's my job. Mildred said for me to do it. Stop interfering."

For a few seconds she glared at Felicia, her fists clenched, and for a brief moment Felicia had the feeling that the elderly woman was about to strike her. She flinched, Lila turned away and the moment passed.

As the evening progressed she had been vaguely aware of Lila's snappy retorts. But she hadn't focused on them because Cora was the center of attention. Too, her mind had been on Harry and the unpleasant manner in which they had parted. But she was beginning to think Lila didn't like her. That's silly, she chided herself. Lila was just trying her wings. Besides, Lila had downed a couple of cups of Clare's laced coffee. Some people just didn't hold their liquor well.

A wind had sprung up, making the candle flames flicker, shadows moved in undulating patterns. Sadie reached out and pinched out the candles with her fingers.

"Waste not, want not," she said, then laughed.

"That was one of my mother's favorite sayings," Felicia said. Then, emotions she'd held in check all evening bubbled up. She blinked back tears. She told Lila good-night and as she wandered upstairs she had the distinct feeling the message in her chart was right. It had been a day of reckoning.

If only on the landscape of her mind.

HARRY FUMED and thrummed his fingers on the steering column. Stuck in traffic. Of all times for there to be a damned wreck. He could see the flashing lights a quarter mile ahead. He kept trying to merge out of the fast lanes into the slower right-hand lanes and thus to the verge where he could make better time. Each time he was cut off.

He kept telling himself Felicia was safe. She was in the backyard at the welcome home party for Cora. She was among friends. Alphonse and Clare and Mildred were all there.

And Lila.

There was no reason for him to have an anxiety attack. It was just a matter of alerting Felicia and the others to Lila's true nature, or other nature. He'd have a word with Ernest Ross, too. Alert him to the little games his mother was playing. Lila needed to be under supervision.

Unbidden memories of the gory photographs of Percy flickered into his mind.

All of his illusions evaporated.

Felicia was at risk. He could feel it in his bones.

The lane he was in began to move, at first slowly because those who passed the pileup rubbernecked. Finally a state trooper was signaling him—Go! Go!

SADIE HUMMED to herself. She had to admit, those old dance tunes Mildred played over and over did have a catchy beat.

Maybe she'd take Mildred up on her offer to play Scrabble later. Of course, Mildred had thought she was asking Lila.

Sadie giggled with a stupendous degree of delight.

The laughter died in her throat.

She had something to do first.

She ticked off the items arrayed on the bed. There was the rubber apron, the knife—how it gleamed! And the stack of mail. Somehow it wasn't quite enough, she brooded.

She went to the dresser, pulled out the bottom drawer and retrieved an aged cigar box from beneath layers of pressed pillow slips where she had hidden it from Lila.

She opened the lid and sniffed. The smell of tobacco was faint. Tampa Nugget Cigars. Papa's favorite. Lila never guessed, but Sadie had always been Papa's special girl. He'd said so. He even played along and called her Sadie.

Not Mama, though. Mama had said Sadie was a figment of Lila's imagination. Mama was wrong! She was here, wasn't she?

She lifted out the tissue-wrapped necklace. Poor Lila. She was so easy to fool.

The opals were milky and glittering.

Sadie hooked them around her neck. Their cool weight sent a small thrill coursing through her. The opals were here, now and forever.

It served Lila right. Mama had always indulged Lila, spoiling her so that she never wanted to share— anything. Not her ribbons, or her fancy dresses, or her socks with the pink lace. Or Percy.

Oh, how she had adored Percy. If he had married her instead of Lila there wouldn't have been any reason for him to bed hop. Certainly he'd have had no use for a mistress.

Once she'd tried to lure Percy to her bed, but he'd slapped her, told her she was acting like a silly old has-been whore. Then he'd laughed.

He'd stopped laughing when she stuck the knife in him.

The knife. Sadie picked it up and stored it deep in a pocket. She tied the apron on. Then she picked up the stack of letters addressed to Felicia Bennington.

She emerged from her apartment, tingling with anticipation.

Chapter Fourteen

When the knock came Felicia's reflection upon intriguing fantasy scenarios was interrupted. Harry had asked her out to dinner and they had actually managed to order and eat without an argument, without a fist fight and without delivering a subpoena. Afterward they had gone for a walk and ended up in her apartment, sipping wine and talking about the future. Their future. Together.

She answered the door, expectant, anticipating Harry. She was smiling.

"Lila." She heard the disappointment in her tone and was at once apologetic. "I'm sorry. I didn't mean to sound—"

"You were expecting someone else?" Sadie pushed her way in and around Felicia.

"I thought it might be Harry," she answered, racking her brain for recall of having issued Lila an invitation. Anything could've slipped past her at the party while she'd been daydreaming of Harry. "Did you need something?"

"What you do with men is evil. Having them up here and taking them away from their wives. That's not nice."

Felicia moaned inwardly. The old, shy, soft-spoken Lila was much preferable to this new, indignant, overbearing one. "Harry isn't married," she said smiling, and stifling a more defiant response to the slur. "Neither am I. We haven't done anything morally wrong." She felt a squeak of conscience. "Not really."

"Percy was married. He was married to Lila."

Percy was married to... What in the world? Had Lila gone off the deep end, or regressed? "I don't know anyone named Percy."

"That's your story." Sadie remembered the letters in her hand. "I brought you these."

Felicia took the batch of mail and glanced at it. "Why, this is a week's worth of my mail. Gosh. How did you get it?"

Sadie laughed tonelessly. "That's for me to know and you to find out."

That was an immature response, Felicia thought. Like something a child would say. "Lila, what's going on?"

"I'm not Lila. Lila's gone. You hurt Lila's feelings." There was implied threat in her voice.

Felicia faltered as the woman transfixed her with a furious scowl. "I haven't hurt anyone," she said guardedly. The old dear had really lost it this time, she thought. Something, somewhere in Lila's brain had turned to mush. The confusion and gibberish Lila was mouthing was so like her mother's before she died, Felicia's heart went out to the old woman. "Why don't we go downstairs and talk with Mildred?" she asked soothingly.

Sadie shook her head. "No. You have to be punished." The last word was little more than a sibilant burst of breath.

Felicia noted the strange glint in the other woman's eyes and felt a tiny stab of fear, then discounted it. Heavens. Lila was an old woman, hardly what one would describe as dangerous. Disturbed, yes, but not dangerous. Maybe Lila was drunk. People under the influence sometimes behaved oddly. Still, it was obvious the situation called for more expertise than she had. She began to ease toward the door. "I'll just call down for Mildred or Alphonse. We'll have coffee and talk this out. How's that?"

Sadie sensed her quarry was about to escape. "No!" she said, and rushed at Felicia with a savage, triumphant grunt.

Felicia was jarred off her feet. This can't be happening, she thought, struggling to rise.

Sadie sat on Felicia's abdomen and scrabbled in her pocket for the knife.

Felicia could not make herself lash out at the older woman. It went against all that she had been taught. She quickly scanned her body. Nothing had been broken in the fall to the floor. She pushed at Lila, trying to dislodge her. "Please, Lila," she gasped. "Get off me. You're hurting me. I can't breathe." She banged on the floor to try to get Alphonse's attention.

Lila's hand came up and the blade winked deadly bright.

Felicia wanted to scream but a sudden icy fear closed her throat.

"Punish," Sadie said thickly, her face contorted. She drew her arm up high. It was going to be wonderful, she thought. Just like when she had carved beef and pork for Papa.

Gasping, Felicia pulled away and scooted out from under her attacker's weight. She scrambled to her feet.

"Oh, Lord. I'm sorry to have to do this," Felicia said, and swung the fat sofa cushion in an arc with both hands. It knocked Lila to the floor. Her head glanced off the sturdy coffee table and she collapsed, her arms thrust outward.

Dazed, Felicia sucked air into her lungs, watching, waiting for Lila to leap up.

The door burst open.

Harry took in the scene in a single glance. He bounded across the room and enclosed Felicia in his arms. "Are you okay? Did she hurt you?"

"I had to hit her. She had a knife. She—"

Felicia's narrative was not a model of coherence but Harry had no trouble following it. "You did the right thing," he murmured. He held her a moment longer, then guided her to a stool at the kitchen counter.

He checked Lila's pulse. It was strong. He checked her head. There was a lump, but no gash, no blood. Knocked out. He called the police. Then he went to stand by Felicia, stroking her head and shoulders gently. He was scared to think about what he might have found, might have discovered.

"It was awful. I couldn't believe she was attacking me. Oh, Harry, she just went out of her mind. She kept saying Lila was gone and I have to be punished."

He wrapped her in his arms and held her tight. "I know, sweetheart. I know. You're safe now. The police are on their way."

"I thought it was *you* at the door. I was waiting for you."

"Yeah? You had something you wanted to say?"

She lifted her face to his. "You were right."

"About what?" He wanted her to get specific.

"About everything. I can't live my life looking for what isn't there. I have to live in the present. Oh! Your mother was right, too!"

He groaned. "Don't bring my mother into this."

"She said there was evil lurking at—" She glanced beyond his shoulder, some movement there catching her eye. "Harry!"

He pushed Felicia aside and turned to see Lila struggling to her feet.

"Sadie!" Harry yelled.

Startled at hearing her name, Sadie froze. Harry used the instant to grab her wrists and swing her arms behind her back.

"Get me a pair of nylons," he ordered Felicia.

She hurried into the bath, grabbed a pair hanging from the shower curtain.

Harry wound and twisted them about Sadie's wrists, tying the knot securely. Then he ushered Sadie to a chair and pushed her, not ungently, into it. "Stay put."

The sirens came closer and died at the front of the building.

Sadie sat up straight. Everything had gone wrong. All of her plans... She had to hide from the police! Panicked, she called Lila, coaxing her to emerge. "I got your necklace back," she whispered.

Lila felt the lovely weight of the opals at her throat. She tried to lift her hands to her neck and couldn't. She looked up, startled to see Harry and Felicia. Why, she was in apartment six!

She heard a clattering of footsteps, people pounding up the stairwell. Two policemen appeared on the threshold. "All right, folks, what's the problem?"

Lila whimpered. "Oh Sadie, what have you done now?"

FELICIA HAD ONLY the vaguest recollection of the succeeding hour. She couldn't keep still. She moved around her apartment in a stupor, picking up the scattered mail and putting things in order.

Harry sat on the sofa. She felt his eyes on her and looked up. They spoke the proverbial volumes. She wished Alphonse would leave, but he was still caught up in the excitement and Harry's explanation about Lila and murder and dual personalities. She wasn't quite comprehending it all herself yet.

"I'm so sorry I didn't come when Felicia banged on the floor," said a crestfallen Alphonse. "I thought she and you were...uh..."

"Cora is in a state of shock," said Mildred, barging in through the still-open door. "She just can't believe Lila was Percy Rossini's widow, and that we never guessed! Cora and Percy had a thing for each other for years. He told her he couldn't leave his wife because she was ill. Of course, Cora didn't believe it. She was crushed when he was killed. Her health started going downhill, the arthritis took over and she couldn't negotiate the stairs any longer." She put her arm around Felicia. "Remember? That's when you got this apartment, after Cora moved downstairs." She smiled judicially. "Clare is just going to hate herself for sleeping through all of this!"

"Sleep. That's what I need," Alphonse said. "Come along, Mildred. I think these two youngsters want to be alone."

Oh, bless you, Felicia thought.

Alphonse turned back at the door. "You will maintain a modicum of decorum, won't you?"

"Oh, by all means," Harry agreed dryly.

Once alone with Harry, behind closed doors, Felicia felt suddenly and awkwardly shy. She couldn't make herself cross the room to Harry until he patted the sofa cushion next to him and beckoned her. "Sit."

"That's the kind of order you give a dog."

"I like dogs. Dogs don't try to pick fights. Dogs adore being petted, scratched behind the ears..." He looked at her searchingly, then continued. "I like you better than dogs."

Felicia held up her hands in a gesture of surrender. She sat. He put his arm about her and pressed his lips to the pink shell of her ear. "Are you certain you're all right?" he asked. "When I think what could have happened..."

She was still a little shaky, but his attention was restorative. "I'm fine, but what will happen to Lila? Will she have to go back to Spadra?"

"I imagine her son will put her in a private psychiatric facility." He began to nibble on her ear lobe. "The state won't balk. It hates to admit it made an error."

Felicia enjoyed the moist little forays of his tongue on her neck. "What does all this do to your thesis?"

"Wraps it up with a dynamite ending." He pulled away, allowing an inch or two of space between them. "You want to talk, let's talk. But are you sure you don't have even one little bruise I can kiss and make well?''

Trailing her fingertips down his cheek, she stopped at his lips and looked up at him with her great smoky eyes. "I suppose it wouldn't do any harm to check.''

SHE SHOOK HIM, poked him, shoved him and lifted his left eyelid. "Wake up, Harry! Now!"

"You could blind a person that way," he said groggily. He glanced at the window. Utter darkness. "What time is it?"

"Four-thirty."

"A.m.?"

She switched on the light.

"I'm blinded."

"Sit up. Look," she said, undeterred by his grimace. "I have a letter from my brother!" Her voice rose to a pitch of almost childish excitement. She dangled the letter before his face. "He's alive."

Harry became fully awake. All along he had been bracing himself to comfort Felicia when the letters turned up no trace of her brother. This sudden twist caught him off guard. "Where did you get a letter at four in the morning?" he asked, praying that her hopes weren't being raised by some con artist.

"It was in the stack of mail Lila brought up. I couldn't sleep so I got up to make some cocoa. For something to do while the milk was heating, I glanced through the mail. It was there. Lila had it all week, Harry. I can forgive her anything, attacking me, calling me names, whatever—but if this letter had been lost..."

He pulled her down beside him. "Let me see it."

"I'll read it to you," she said, her voice breathy. "I can visit him. Listen:

Dear Felicia,

Your letter of inquiry was passed on to me in case I wanted to respond. The director of the home thinks I might be coming into some money, but I know there can't be anything left of Mom's and Dad's estate. It was a shock to hear that Mom had died. She told me she was ill the last time she visited and, as her letters came less frequently, then none at all, I suspected the worst, but I still hoped.

You must be devastated. I know how close you and Mom were.

Knowing what I do of you, I suppose you'll insist on visiting me. I won't encourage you, but I won't ask you not to. God bless.

Thomas A. Bennington.

"It sounds authentic," Harry said.

Felicia leaped off the bed. "Do you have suspicions of everybody and everything? I'm getting dressed. I'm going to see him."

"In the middle of the night? Be sensible. Where is he? Around the corner?"

"He's in a full-care center called Magnolia Park a few miles north of Paradise."

"Paradise."

"Why aren't you happy for me? Finding my brother is . . . Don't you know what this means?" Her hands were trembling, her face was flushed. Her eyes burned with an inner anguish. "I have family."

"It means there are two of you loose in the world."

"Get out of my bed and go home."

"Nope. I have no intention of letting you make this trip alone. I'll drive you. Your heap barely makes it to the barns and back."

"Thank you." Her voice was filled with relief. "I'll make us a thermos of coffee for the trip."

Harry stretched and rubbed his eyes. For a few moments he gave himself up to remembering Felicia's hands upon him, more bold than before, seeking to learn and know his body, caressing him, encouraging and moving sensually on him. His eyes drifted closed.

Felicia dropped the road atlas on his chest. His eyes flew open again. "Plot our trip. Here's some coffee. What do you want to wear? I'll go get you some clothes."

"Jeans, a shirt."

"To meet my brother for the first time? Are you mad?"

"I forgot," he teased, grinning. "What were you wearing when you met my mother?"

He won. He wore jeans, a sweatshirt and espadrilles. It was five hundred and twenty-one miles north to Paradise. Felicia felt herself in hell the entire drive. And if not hell, then limbo. "I wonder what he looks like. I wonder what's wrong with him? Suppose he doesn't like me. Suppose he resents me?"

"Suppose you stop worrying," Harry admonished.

"We should've stopped and called to let him know we were coming. Suppose he isn't there? He may be on an outing or something. Do they get outings, I wonder. How much longer, Harry?"

They arrived at 3:52 p.m. The Magnolia Park Nursing Home was a sprawling single-story building set far back in a grove of loblolly pine. Ironically, there wasn't a magnolia tree in sight. It had a shady verandah on the south side, furnished with a long row of rocking chairs.

Harry tried to pry Felicia from the car.

"My stomach's queasy."

He started the engine again.

"What're you *doing*?"

"Going home."

She put her hand on his. "Will you go in with me?"

"I wouldn't miss this for the world." He dreaded being a spectator, but if Felicia was ever going to be wholly his, the issue of Thomas Adam Bennington, twin, had to be resolved. He wanted her rid of the niggling fear of commitment, wanted her to learn that she was a person in her own right—if only for his own decidedly nonaltruistic reasons. He heard his own thoughts and laughed silently. Look whose talking! Damn it all! Had he ever come full circle. Well, he should've guessed it'd happen—he wasn't equipped for casual liaisons.

He gripped Felicia's elbow and guided her into the building.

The reception area was an empty desk, behind which was a sprawling recreation area. Several people in wheelchairs were parked in front of a television. Two old men played checkers at a table.

Felicia gripped Harry's arm as she scanned the room. She saw no one who could possibly be her brother.

One of the old men looked up, smiled and waved them over. "You visiting?" he asked.

Felicia could only nod. Harry spoke. "We're looking for Thomas Bennington."

"Down corridor B, just follow the yellow line. Last room on the right. Oh, but sign the guest book first. Matron always likes to know who's in the building. It's on the desk."

Felicia signed their names in a shaky scrawl. Corridor B might as well have been a dark and unlighted tunnel. She focused only on the last door on the right. It was open. She felt sweat beading down her back. Almost there. One more step. Harry shook her gently.

"Don't go catatonic on me. A slow breath, okay."

"I'm fine."

She stepped to the threshold and looked in. Thomas Adam Bennington was sitting up in bed, a sketch pad attached to a contraption that held it at the correct angle for him. His eyes lifted. For a moment he was utterly still, as if frozen in time, then his eyes lit up and he smiled. "Hello, Felicia. I knew you'd come."

It was her own smile, she saw, her own gray eyes. He was smaller of bone and build than she, or perhaps he was made to seem so by the hospital bed. His features were angular, as if assembled from an assortment of geometric pieces. Similar to her own, but far more masculine. His hair was dark, brushed straight back. He had a widow's peak, like their father.

She quickly scanned the room. It was little more than a closet, its single saving grace an eight-foot window through which the sunlight poured in. The walls were covered in photographs of herself, of her parents and sketches of waiflike whimsical creatures.

She spoke. "You're an artist, too?"

"Not on the scale you are." His gaze went to Harry. "This is Harry Pritchard. He drove..."

Harry ushered Felicia fully into the room. Tom thrust out his hand toward him. Harry murmured a greeting, accepted Tom's hand and found the grip surprisingly strong.

"I'm called Tom. Used to be Tommy, but I rebelled after I turned twenty-five." He gestured to Felicia to sit on the foot of his bed, Harry to take the single chair. "Unless you'd like to go outside? I can call an attendant to bring a wheelchair."

"No...no. This is fine," she said, settling herself at his direction. She felt...she didn't know how she felt—awkward. But this was her brother! His eyes were glued to her.

He laughed. "You look as though you're at your own execution."

Felicia smiled. "I feel it."

"You must have a thousand questions."

Felicia broke. "Why didn't Mom and Dad tell me about you? You knew about me!" she wailed, indicating the photos that covered the walls.

"They didn't expect me to live. There were a lot more things wrong than just deformed hipbones and legs. My insides weren't right. A heart murmur. There was surgery to connect my intestines to my stomach, my spleen was removed. Infections. Always something. I just happened to be one tough cookie. Good old Bennington stock, I guess."

"That's not an answer. It's been thirty years! How could Mom and Dad keep you a secret?"

"They weren't ashamed of me, if that's what you're driving at. In a way they were protecting me. There was no way Mom and Dad could've taken care of me at home. I needed full-time care." He smiled. "Still do. We talked about you a lot. We talked about telling you, wondered about how you'd feel. You can't take care of me, Felicia. I didn't want you to be burdened. Mom and Dad had enough guilt. When Mom got sick she begged me to allow her to tell you I existed. I refused."

"But, I always knew! I sensed you existed."

He smiled. "Mom told me you drove her wild with that—your alter ego. Asking why the hidden person inside you was lost?"

"When did they see you? Where was I?"

"Early on you were home with neighbors. Later, don't you recall Dad taking trips, Mom sometimes going with him. You spent the night with your girlfriends. Of course, once you went away to college, Mom was free to visit more often. And once you were busy doing the Rose Parade floats, we spent Christmas together—here."

"But you must've been so lonely!"

"Nope. Besides, I work." He handed her the sketch pad. "I illustrate children's books. Once, I did a coloring book—jungle animals. The pay isn't fabulous, but I can't make huge sums anyway or my benefits would be scaled back. I make spending money."

Felicia flipped through the book. The scene he was working on was a bevy of forest animals racing to hide from a puppy. "You're talented."

Tom glowed. "High praise, coming from an award-winning float designer. I'm honored." He turned to Harry. "How did you and Felicia meet?"

"She accused me of theft."

Felicia protested. Harry cut her off. "The man was talking to me."

Tom grinned. "When are you two tying the knot?"

"In a couple of weeks," Harry said. "Wanna come?"

Felicia's mouth fell open.

"Sure. I can get a pass—and a nurse, if you can provide transportation."

"Can do," Harry said, glancing at Felicia out of the corner of his eye. His every instinct told him to clear out now. "Any place a guy can get a soft drink around here? I'm dying of thirst."

Tom gave him directions to the cafeteria.

As he left Felicia murmured, "Thirst isn't all you're going to die of." But when she turned back to Tom, she was unsure of herself and at a complete loss for words.

He laughed. "Something tells me marriage had not been mentioned until I stuck my foot in it."

Felicia pumped up a mild anger. "You have the advantage over me. You know all about me. I feel like I'm trying to make friends with my own brother, that I'm on approval, and then Harry goes and—" She didn't want to cry. She wanted to hold the tears in reserve until she was alone. They came anyway.

Tom didn't try to stop her.

After a few moments she brushed away the tears, searched her purse for a tissue and blew her nose. "Sorry. That was stupid of me."

"I didn't think so. Tell me, how was Mom at the last." He sighed. "I miss her. It was hard on me when Dad died, but this is worse somehow. I expected Mom to live forever or at the least, to outlive me."

"God! I hadn't given that a thought." Just as she felt the burning dryness in her eyes, the tears began to flow again. "You must feel...I've been so selfish! Thinking only of myself. I have to keep remembering Mom was your mom, too." She hiccuped.

Tom continued as if she hadn't spoken, prodding her until she launched into details of their mother's last weeks and the funeral. She discovered the telling was somehow cathartic. Tom was, after all, family. She went on to regale him with the story of finding the birth certificate, Zelda, Thea and Harry, and an edited version of Lila and her life at the Catalina Arms.

When Harry returned, they were so engrossed with getting to know each other, he stayed in the background, reluctant to intrude upon the territorial integrity of brother-sister, of family.

But he watched and he listened. Tom and Felicia's laugh was the same, their hand gestures and mobile features remarkably in sync. He realized he was watching Felicia's inner core emerge—she bloomed.

The possibility that Tom might become his brother-in-law got him to thinking.

He and Tom might never play touch football together, dribble a basketball or jog along the beach. But the man had intellect. And he'd be a good mind to bounce investigative theories off. It was something to look forward to.

They stayed for supper, eating in the brightly painted cafeteria at a large round table that accommodated wheelchairs. A young nurse's aide joined them. Conversation was light and witty and to Harry's dismay, never touched on marriage.

Felicia sat upright and silent the first fifty miles going home.

Finally Harry took the bit in his mouth. "Okay. Here's my idea. We could get our blood tests on Monday, our license on Tuesday. Or—we can pop over to Vegas and do it in one of those wedding chapels."

Silence.

"You didn't expect me to get down on my knees, did you? Hell, I'd never get up."

Felicia exhaled audibly, leaned her head back and closed her eyes, ignoring him.

"Want to stop?" he asked playfully. "Spend the night in a motel?"

"You could've asked me. But, no—"

"Maybe I thought it'd just get filed with all your other proposals. Or that if I gave you time to think about it, you'd turn me down."

"Oh, sure, there're a dozen hopeful grooms beating a path to my door." In the glow of lights from the dash her skin was unnaturally pale. Harry noticed the faint blue shadows under her eyes that underscored the trauma and excitement she'd gone through in the past two days.

He pulled into the parking area of a scenic overlook and cut the motor. Then he reached over and brushed her cheek with his fingers. Her skin felt cool. "All right," he said cautiously, "I'll chance it. Will you marry me?"

She looked up into the sky. There was a sliver of moon. Beyond the scenic overlook, a valley spread out deep and shadowy. She had a shock of realization. A real shock. Yesterday she would've likened her life to those deep and dark shadows. But the peculiar questing sense, the search for the lost child within her had been exorcised. As for the rest—her doubts about her ability to maintain relationships, the sense of aloneness, her fears—all had dissipated.

Of course she was going to marry Harry.

It was meant to be.

"Damn it, Felicia," Harry said. "Say something."

"Marriage is unpredictable, challenging and hazardous..."

Harry groaned.

Felicia grinned. "I wear a size-five ring."

Chapter Fifteen

Harry woke late in the afternoon. He showered, dressed and went to find Felicia.

There was a post-it note on her door addressed to him.

Zelda's back. We've gone shopping. My chart predicts July twenty-second is a good day to get married, three in the afternoon.

Harry went to see his mother.

"You have your astrology books handy?"

"Always, dear boy. Why?"

"On the off chance that I might want to, what would be a good day for me to get married?"

Thea opened one of her books and began to pencil in notations and figures. She looked at Harry and smiled. "August seventh, in the morning."

Harry groaned. "Suppose I got married on July twenty-second at three in the afternoon?"

"That would be better for me. I'll be in Florida in August."

"Mom, get serious."

"I am serious. Now, Harry, we've never talked about this, but I've always felt that the ten thousand dollars your father left us was your legacy as well as mine. I just put it to use for us both. Now that I've sold the store, I'm giving you half of what I'm getting for it."

"What are the long-range consequences of me getting married July twenty-second?"

"Harry, dear, you are always going to be stubborn and excitable. However, if Felicia insists on July twenty-second, I think you should agree."

"Who said anything about Felicia?"

"She did. She called me. Among other things, we discussed the rehearsal dinner. And, Harry, I implore you, don't ask too many of your disreputable friends. We will not be serving beer."

Harry sputtered. "She hasn't discussed a rehearsal dinner with me!"

"She doesn't need to, sweet son of mine—you're only the groom. However, she's made it clear you are very much the object of her affection, and I approve."

Back at the Catalina Arms he found Felicia on the front steps, her arms encircling a cardboard box. A moving van was parked at the curb. Harry's heart lurched. Murphy's Law! he thought. Something was wrong. Felicia was leaving. He took the box from her arms and put it on the sidewalk. "What is it? What's happened?"

She sniffed. "Ernest is here. We're all helping him clear out Lila's apartment."

Harry wanted to protect her from every bad and unhappy thing in the world. He pulled her into his arms. "Don't even think about it."

"I just feel so bad for Lila. Ernest *did* put her in a private psychiatric hospital. Mildred and Clare are going to go see her when she's allowed visitors. Ernest said I shouldn't go."

"He's right," Harry agreed, stilling a shudder against thoughts of what might have been. He smiled down at her. "Tell you what, I'll help load Lila's things, you go freshen up. I'm taking you out for a celebration dinner."

"Oh, Harry, I can't. We're going through all of Mildred's wedding outfits to see if something can be made over for me."

"Okay. Suppose I order Chinese for later. We can—"

"Zelda is spending the next few nights. She's going to be my maid of honor and help with the bridal showers. Clare is giving me one and so is Grady's wife—you know, the float engineer—"

Harry frowned. "What about me? When are we going to have some time together?"

Felicia smiled. "You are kind and principled and intelligent, Harry—but I don't want you anywhere near my wedding preparations."

"That hurts my feelings. It's my wedding, too."

"Okay. You provide one best man in a cutaway tux, one wedding band, plain gold, please, and yourself promptly at 3:00 p.m. July twenty-second at the foot of the fire escape. Mildred is baking the groom's cake." She gave him a peck on the cheek. "Go tell her whether you want carrot cake or chocolate. Oh, and since you're so thick with Cooper—get him to provide a platform of sorts. Alphonse insists on giving me away. Tom's going to do the pictures." She took a breath.

"That's all?"

"You could finish typing your thesis. I don't want it coming between us on our honeymoon."

"We're going on a honeymoon?"

"Aren't we? That's the groom's department. You pick the place."

"Can't you think of anything else?"

He watched her checking lists in her mind. "Alphonse is going with you to get your blood test. Zelda's going with me. I'll meet you at the courthouse to pick up the marriage license."

"Your efficiency boggles my mind," he said glumly. "Just be sure you hold the weekend open for me—for us."

Felicia reached up and took his face in her hands. She planted a kiss full of promise on his lips. "Sorry— that's out, too. Your mother and I are driving up to see Tom. She wants to meet him."

"But—"

HE RECEIVED an A-minus on his thesis.

Fred Lawson sucked on his pipe and smiled a superior smile around the stem. "Excellent. Would've pulled an A, but you only provided your own observations for the wrap on the Rossini case. There should be a couple of good articles in this," he added.

"Three," said Harry.

"Oh?" The pipe dangled.

California Bar Journal, the *Review* and *True Detective*. I'm using a pseudonym for *True Detective*. The editor said that'd be all right," Harry added blandly, leaning back, his legs crossed.

"I see," Lawson said, his tone frigid.

"Hope so," said Harry and let himself out.

Felicia and his mother took him to dinner to celebrate.

"Fill me in," Thea said, once he'd recapped the thesis for her. "How did Clare hide the money?"

"Cleverly, but I'm obliged not to discuss it until Alphonse...uh...why don't you look it up in her horoscope?"

Thea peered at him over the rim of her brandy glass. "That's not an answer designed to strengthen the bonds of maternal affection, Harry, dear. His naughty mouth comes from his Dad, not me," she informed Felicia.

Beneath the table Felicia held hands with Harry. "He's not so bad. I like him."

Harry would have preferred she used a stronger word.

At the Catalina Arms he pulled her down on the top stair before she could escape into her apartment. "Like? You like me? That's all? If we're getting married there better be more than like."

She snuggled against him. "I adore you. You're romantic, handsome and the best thing that has ever happened to me."

His hand traveled up her leg. "Felicia, we're either going to have to fight about this or make love. I'm tired of being apart."

"Two more days," she whispered. "Only two."

"Do I hear a touch of longing in your voice?"

She laughed weakly. "More than a touch. The dreams I have of you are positively wicked."

"That's all right then. I thought I was in pain all by myself."

SHE WAS STILL in all her wedding finery: peach-colored silk sheath, pearls on loan from Clare and small-brimmed hat with the short veil tossed back. She looked like a sun-ripened peach, Harry thought. Moist, juicy and warm. He was ready to take a long and lazy sample.

A highly agitated Alphonse tapped Harry on the shoulder. "I do hate to disturb the bride and groom, but, Harry, could I have a word with you?"

"Sure. What's—"

"Who is that Manny gentleman who keeps pouring champagne down Clare's throat?"

Felicia laughed. "Why, Alphonse. I think you're jealous."

"I should say I'm not." He shot his heavily starched French cuffs. "But Clare's behavior is exceedingly unladylike, perhaps you'd better have a word with her."

Harry put his arm around Alphonse. "Sorry, old sport, but you'll have to work for your woman like I did."

"I should reduce myself to chasing her?"

Harry grinned. "Crawl, if that's what it takes."

For a brief instant Alphonse paled. "I really don't care how she hid the money, you know. But she's been a virgin for so long, it's a milestone she ought not to give up lightly."

"That's a lovely way of putting it," Felicia said. "Go tell her that."

"Then what?" Alphonse asked, confused.

"Call Manny a cab and send him home. He's on his last legs anyhow."

"Felicia!" Zelda called. "When are you going to throw your bouquet?"

"Right now!" She took Harry's hand. "Let's get up on the fire escape."

Together they ran back through the wedding guests: Thea, Clare, Mildred, Cora; Harry's former colleagues and their wives; the judge who had married them; various float designers and engineers; Tom in a wheelchair surrounded by admirers of his works in progress, which were renditions of the wedding party—perfect replicas of each face atop a suitably whimsical jungle animal. Felicia knew she'd treasure the sketches for years to come.

She and Harry stopped midway up the fire escape. "I love you all," she cried and turned around, tossing the bouquet over her shoulder. There were squeals and shouts of glee. The nurse who accompanied Tom caught the flowers and blushed.

Felicia started down the steps. Harry held her back. "Nope. This way." He guided her up to the landing.

The look on his face was one of fierce determination. Felicia balked. "Harry, we can't. Everyone will know."

"By my count and it's accurate as hell, in the past twenty-one days I've only had you to myself for one hour and forty-five minutes. That's a lot of time to make up for. We're starting right now."

He scooped her up and carried her over his windowsill to a roar of catcalls and whistles. He pulled down the window, then the shade.

"You're impossible," Felicia said. "But, you're my impossible." She put her arms around his neck and whispered. "I love you, Harry Pritchard."

FELICIA PROPPED herself up on her pillows. Something had awakened her. Harry was beside her, his head nestled in a pillow, his arm lying across her waist. Mrs. Harry Pritchard, she thought, smiling. The noise came again. A series of thuds coming from downstairs.

Carefully she moved Harry's arm and swung her legs over the side of the bed. She looked out the window. "Oh! Harry! Wake up!"

He mumbled.

She shook him. "Wake up. There's something going on with your car downstairs."

"Hell!" he muttered, getting up and pulling on his tux pants.

Felicia shrugged into his robe and followed him down the fire escape.

At the foot of the steps they met Alphonse. Clare, wearing Alphonse's smoking jacket over her nightgown, came rushing out of Alphonse's apartment.

The couples stared at one another for a moment.

"We thought you were leaving," said Clare. "We came out to throw the rice."

"We fell asleep," said Harry.

"We didn't," said Clare, giggling.

Harry looked at his bride. "Is this what you woke me up for?"

"No." Felicia flung her arm toward the back of fence. "They're towing your car out of the alley. We forgot—"

But Harry was already loping off.

"If you'll excuse us," Alphonse said, taking Clare's arm.

Clare's giggling innuendo registered with Felicia. "Hold on a minute, Clare. It seems you got what you wanted. So out with it. How did you hide the money?"

"Oh, it was easy as pie. I took the cash and bought war bonds. Then I recorded their numbers behind servicemen's names in my address book as if the numbers were service serial numbers. Then I burned the bonds. Simple. No evidence. You can replace them, you know. I learned that working for Wells Fargo. You don't even have to have the serial numbers, but it makes it easier. Nobody ever suspects savings bonds. They always look for secret bank accounts or hidden safety deposit boxes. Like Alphonse did."

"Yep, that's what I did."

Clare laughed gleefully. "After I got out of prison and got all the bonds replaced, I cashed each and every one as I needed it at Wells Fargo. They have a female vice-president now. I like to think I paved her way." She tugged at Alphonse. "C'mon, let's fiddle around some more before Mildred wakes up and comes looking for me." She turned back and showered Felicia with a handful of rice. "Just in case we're not around when you and Harry get off on your honeymoon."

Felicia sat on the bottom step of the fire escape, brushed rice out of her hair and waited for Harry.

He came limping into the garden.

"Did you catch up to the tow truck?"

"Yep. He's putting the car around front."

"What'd it cost you?"

"Seeing as how I'm a newlywed—ten bucks . . ."

Felicia laughed. "Life with you is going to be an adventure."

". . . and breakfast."

"Breakfast? What? Who?"

"The tow-truck guy. Don't get upset. He's been working all night—"

"Harry, husband of mine . . . you go meet that guy at the front door and give him another ten dollars so he can feed himself. We have other plans for breakfast."

"We do?"

She put her arms around his neck and nibbled on his ear.

"I guess we do," Harry said happily.

New Year's Day

The staging area for the parade was a cacophony of sound and smell. Marching bands tuned up, horses neighed; costumed men, women and children who were to mount the floats milled about by the hundreds. Engineers, designers and float builders gave their entries last-minute once-overs. Harry stood amid the throng in numbed dismay. He'd never find Felicia in all this chaos. The only sight that gave him any comfort was the herd of uniformed motorcycle patrolman outriders who were beginning to drive out onto Colorado Boulevard to manage crowd control.

He spotted her. Damn it! She was perched precariously atop a step ladder doing something to the nose of a huge animated puppy. He pushed through a group of volunteers carrying boxes of pink carnations. Fearful of startling her and making her lose her balance, he climbed up the first few steps of the ladder below her. She looked down.

"Hi."

"Hi, my Aunt Ethel. Get off this thing. You promised me you wouldn't do anything reckless."

"This isn't reckless. Pass me that box of onion seed. This little guy's nose got wacked. I'll get down as soon as it's fixed."

Harry handed her the seeds silently. She patted them into the glue and leaned back to inspect the repair. Harry felt a stab of fear that she would topple backward. He put his hand on her back to support her.

Felicia sighed. "That feels good. I could use a back rub." She allowed him to help her down. "Did you pick your mother up from the airport?"

"I did everything—Mother's with Cora and Tom in the viewing stands, I escorted Alphonse and Clare and Mildred to the corner you told me to, and set up their chairs. And everyone has directions to the house for afterward. What I want to know is when I can take you home?"

"As soon as all my floats have pulled out. My last one is number thirty-four."

He put his hand on her belly. "How's this little fellow doing?"

Felicia put her hand over Harry's and grinned. "I think he's been playing soccer with his little brother or sister." She waited and watched for the comment to register. Harry went white around the lips.

"His what?"

"The doctor called me at the barns yesterday morning. Looks like there are going to be two little Pritchards making their debut in March."

"But...how?"

Felicia bit back her laughter at his stunned reaction. "I guess these things run in families. You're stuck, Harry."

"And you're okay? The babies are okay?"

"We are all perfectly fine."

He took her face in his hands. "Then, so am I, Mrs. Pritchard. I can handle it."

"Want to come with me to check on my other float?"

He put his arm around her expanding waist. "I want to come with you wherever you go."

"Even into the delivery room?"

Harry felt a sudden balloon of air in his gut. "I—" He recalled his horoscope. The day starts off in a promising way and ends up with a happy surprise, but the part in between could bring some edgy moments.

This was his edgy moment. "I'll be there," he said firmly.

As if she were reading his mind, Felicia said, "My horoscope said today would auger well for my personal dreams. That they would show signs of coming true."

Harry's amber eyes narrowed to slits. "And?"

She slipped her hand into his. "It was right on target. My dreams have come true."

H·I·S·T·O·R·I·C·A·L
Christmas
S·T·O·R·I·E·S 1·9·9·0

Once again Harlequin, the experts in
romance, bring you the magic of Christmas
—as celebrated in America's past.

These enchanting love stories
celebrate Christmas made extra-
special by the wonder of people
in love....

Nora Roberts	**In From the Cold**
Patricia Potter	**Miracle of the Heart**
Ruth Langan	**Christmas at Bitter Creek**

Look for this Christmas title next month
wherever Harlequin® books are sold.

"Makes a great stocking stuffer."

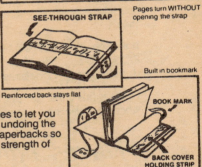

PASSPORT TO ROMANCE VACATION SWEEPSTAKES

OFFICIAL RULES

SWEEPSTAKES RULES AND REGULATIONS. NO PURCHASE NECESSARY.

HOW TO ENTER:

1. To enter, complete this official entry form and return with your invoice in the envelope provided, or print your name, address, telephone number and age on a plain piece of paper and mail to: Passport to Romance, P.O. Box #1397, Buffalo, N.Y. 14269-1397. No mechanically reproduced entries accepted.
2. All entries must be received by the Contest Closing Date, midnight, December 31, 1990 to be eligible.
3. Prizes: There will be ten (10) Grand Prizes awarded, each consisting of a choice of a trip for two people to: i) London, England (approximate retail value $5,050 U.S.); ii) England, Wales and Scotland (approximate retail value $6,400 U.S.); iii) Caribbean Cruise (approximate retail value $7,300 U.S.); iv) Hawaii (approximate retail value $ 9,550 U.S.); v) Greek Island Cruise in the Mediterranean (approximate retail value $12,250 U.S.); vi) France (approximate retail value $7,300 U.S.).
4. Any winner may choose to receive any trip or a cash alternative prize of $5,000.00 U.S. in lieu of the trip.
5. Odds of winning depend on number of entries received.
6. A random draw will be made by Nielsen Promotion Services, an independent judging organization on January 29, 1991, in Buffalo, N.Y., at 11:30 a.m. from all eligible entries received on or before the Contest Closing Date. Any Canadian entrants who are selected must correctly answer a time-limited, mathematical skill-testing question in order to win. Quebec residents may submit any litigation respecting the conduct and awarding of a prize in this contest to the Régie des loteries et courses du Quebec.
7. Full contest rules may be obtained by sending a stamped, self-addressed envelope to: "Passport to Romance Rules Request", P.O. Box 9998, Saint John, New Brunswick, E2L 4N4.
8. Payment of taxes other than air and hotel taxes is the sole responsibility of the winner.
9. Void where prohibited by law.

PASSPORT TO ROMANCE VACATION SWEEPSTAKES

OFFICIAL RULES

SWEEPSTAKES RULES AND REGULATIONS. NO PURCHASE NECESSARY.

HOW TO ENTER:

1. To enter, complete this official entry form and return with your invoice in the envelope provided, or print your name, address, telephone number and age on a plain piece of paper and mail to: Passport to Romance, P.O. Box #1397, Buffalo, N.Y. 14269-1397. No mechanically reproduced entries accepted.
2. All entries must be received by the Contest Closing Date, midnight, December 31, 1990 to be eligible.
3. Prizes: There will be ten (10) Grand Prizes awarded, each consisting of a choice of a trip for two people to: i) London, England (approximate retail value $5,050 U.S.); ii) England, Wales and Scotland (approximate retail value $6,400 U.S.); iii) Caribbean Cruise (approximate retail value $7,300 U.S.); iv) Hawaii (approximate retail value $ 9,550 U.S.); v) Greek Island Cruise in the Mediterranean (approximate retail value $12,250 U.S.); vi) France (approximate retail value $7,300 U.S.).
4. Any winner may choose to receive any trip or a cash alternative prize of $5,000.00 U.S. in lieu of the trip.
5. Odds of winning depend on number of entries received.
6. A random draw will be made by Nielsen Promotion Services, an independent judging organization on January 29, 1991, in Buffalo, N.Y., at 11:30 a.m. from all eligible entries received on or before the Contest Closing Date. Any Canadian entrants who are selected must correctly answer a time-limited, mathematical skill-testing question in order to win. Quebec residents may submit any litigation respecting the conduct and awarding of a prize in this contest to the Régie des loteries et courses du Quebec.
7. Full contest rules may be obtained by sending a stamped, self-addressed envelope to: "Passport to Romance Rules Request", P.O. Box 9998, Saint John, New Brunswick, E2L 4N4.
8. Payment of taxes other than air and hotel taxes is the sole responsibility of the winner.
9. Void where prohibited by law.

PASSPORT TO ROMANCE
WIN
1 of 10 Vacations
SEE INSIDE

VACATION SWEEPSTAKES

MONTH 2 ENTRY

Official Entry Form

Yes, enter me in the drawing for one of ten Vacations-for-Two! If I'm a winner, I'll get my choice of any of the six different destinations being offered — and I won't have to decide until after I'm notified!

Return entries with invoice in envelope provided along with Daily Travel Allowance Voucher. Each book in your shipment has two entry forms — and the more you enter, the better your chance of winning!

Name _____

Address _____ Apt. ____

City _____ State/Prov. _____ Zip/Postal Code

Daytime phone number _____
Area Code

☐ I am enclosing a Daily Travel
Allowance Voucher in the amount of $_____ . _____ Write in amount
revealed beneath scratch-off

CPS-TWO

"You see, we mortals are so pompous that we have deluded ourselves into believing that in all of eternity, and all of the vast universe, that we are the only ones who have undergone the human experience. I've always believed that it's happened before, on this very earth."

"Here . . . how . . . ?"

"Well, in God's scheme what is a few billion years, here and there. Perhaps there have come and gone a dozen human civilizations in the past billion years that we know nothing about. And after this civilization we are living in destroys itself, it will all start up again in a few hundred million years when the planet has all its messes cleaned up. Then, finally, one of these civilizations, say five billion years from now, will last for eternity because people will treat each other the way they ought to."

They were interrupted by the phone. Abe's face became very tense. He wrote out an address and said he would come over within the hour. He set the receiver down, puzzled.

"That was Terrence Campbell. He wants to see me."

"Well, that shouldn't surprise you. You see, if we are going to hang on to this world for a little longer it's going to be up to him and Kelno's son and your son and daughter. Well, I shan't hold you up any longer. How long will you be about?"

"I'm leaving for Israel in a few days. Back where I started, as a journalist."

They shook hands. "I can't say you've been my most restrained client, but it's been interesting," Bannister said, unable to find words in one of the rare instances in his life. "You know what I mean."

"I know what you mean, Tom."

"Good luck, Abe."

ON THE WAY TO SEE TERRENCE I ASKED THE TAXI TO STOP AT THE LAW COURT. WELL, THAT'S NATURAL. TO SAY GOOD-BY TO THE ONE DECENT THING I'VE DONE IN MY LIFE, FIGHT THIS CASE.

I CANNOT SHAKE BANNISTER'S NOTION THAT THERE

HAVE BEEN CIVILIZATIONS BEFORE US, AND IT WILL
HAPPEN AGAIN. WHEN THIS ONE GOES, I'M GOING TO BE
VERY SORRY ABOUT LONDON.

DOWN THE STREET FROM THE LAW COURT IS ST.
CLEMENT DANES CHURCH. IT'S THE ROYAL AIR FORCE
CHURCH, AND I KNEW IT WELL DURING THE WAR. IN
FACT, I WROTE SOME COLUMNS ABOUT IT.

ST. CLEMENT DANES IS EXACTLY WHAT THOMAS BAN-
NISTER WAS TALKING ABOUT. IT WAS BUILT BY THE
DANES IN 871 OR THEREABOUTS WHEN KING ALFRED
EXPELLED THEM BEYOND THE CITY WALL AND THEN IT
WAS DESTROYED. IT WAS REBUILT BY WILLIAM THE
CONQUEROR, AND DESTROYED, AND REBUILT IN THE
MIDDLE AGES AND DESTROYED IN THE FIRE OF 1666,
AND REBUILT, AND DESTROYED IN 1680 AND REBUILT
BY CHRISTOPHER WREN, AND STOOD UNTIL THE GER-
MAN BOMBERS DESTROYED IT IN THE SECOND WORLD
WAR. AND IT WAS REBUILT AGAIN.

WHAT THE HELL'S THAT NURSERY RHYME SAMANTHA
USED TO TELL THE CHILDREN?

ORANGES AND LEMONS,
SAY THE BELLS OF ST. CLEMENT'S
YOU OWE ME FIVE FARTHINGS
SAY THE BELLS OF ST. MARTIN'S
WHEN WILL YOU PAY ME
SAY THE BELLS OF OLD BAILEY
WHEN I GROW RICH
SAY THE BELLS OF SHOREDITCH
WHEN WILL THAT BE
SAY THE BELLS OF STEPNEY
I DO NOT KNOW
SAY THE GREAT BELLS OF BOW
HERE COMES A COPPER TO PUT YOU TO BED
HERE COMES A CHOPPER TO CHOP OFF YOUR HEAD

Tel Aviv, June 6, 1967 (AP) The Israel Defense Ministry
announced that its casualties were light in the strike that
destroyed the Arab air forces. Most prominent among those
killed was Sergent (Captain) Ben Cady, son of the well-
known author.